A Nasty Piece Of Work*

Graham Bendel

FORTUNE TELLER PRESS

First Edition, published in 2008

by Fortune Teller Press

A Nasty Piece Of Work copyright ©

ISBN: 978 0 9547737 3 1

GW00383971

All rights reserved. No part of this publication may be reproduced, transmitted, or stored in a retrieval system or transmitted in any form or by any means, electronic, mechanical, photocopying, recording or otherwise, without the prior written permission of the publisher. No part of this publication must be used for advertising, sales promotion or publicity.

....

Front cover art by Clive Barker ©. Many thanks to him for that.

ABOUT THE AUTHOR
Graham Bendel is a writer, living in London.
He is the editor of the Poems For The Retired Nihilist series and
the director of the documentary film Billy Childish Is Dead.

Many thanks to: Tim Awford, Alis Cox, Asa Pellijeff,
Will Broadbent and Tina Vaughan for their feedback and comments.

WEBSITE: www.fortunetellerpress.com

A NASTY PIECE OF WORK

(or A Blank Page For The Blind)

By

Graham Bendel

PART 1

CHAPTER NOUGHT

Introduction.

As unpleasant as it might sound: I was intended to hurt her. He said she needed to be in pain, and tortured. Any failure to carry out 'his' order was my immediate death warrant. So I had to comply, you understand.

I know what you're thinking already, this far into this sick story: there was no him. He didn't exist and it is. . .it is with regret that I write out the story of my recent life; and write this (hopefully well?) from the discomfort of my cell.

I write this in the third person for one principal reason: that it makes my mistakes (please God) seem that they were committed by someone else.

I fear that some, who are like me, may not recognise themselves in this story. But remember this: vampires do not ever see their own reflections. I know this now.

My name is Jonathan Urich and 'this story' is all I have left, the need to know you are listening.

CHAPTER ONE

The beginning of the end.

Jonathan Urich, at this point, had no real understanding of Sacrifice.

(But that comes later.)

Urich was a hard-working, tow-the-line type.

He was 'in publishing', working as a literary agent in a small but once-famous agency. And they were going to fire him. Because they wanted some big new novels and he hadn't delivered any. But could he be blamed? All he was getting sent was novels about council estates. Or novels with terribly-named characters based, most likely, on shops on the Tottenham Court Road, or dodgy food products. Last week, he had the misfortune of encountering a drug dealer called "Big Mick Jessop" and an ex-SAS man named "Zak Ginster".

But did his superiors care about how Urich almost felt contaminated by reading this third-rate filth? Sometimes he wanted to take a shower and douse himself in antiseptic.

It was September 1996. He was in the toilet of Bitter Lemon in Hanover Street, snorting mediocre coke and worrying about money, and how he might lose his flat.

"Urine, get your fat arse out of the toilet," Monty Carn complained – greedy for a snifter of Urich's small stash.

But Urich was doing something altogether different, and something unlikely to involve his overweight work colleague. He had decided –on a whim, after taking a post-coke leak – to give himself more than the customary 'three to seven' shakes, and enjoy a frantic one off the wrist. He was thinking about Cynthia again. And Carn was outside the cubicle door being a drunken lout. What's more: he sounded like he was being superior to Urich.

But Monty had reason: he was on the up, and his association with Mike Jones, the political comedian, was a real lifeline. Jones' books sold. Jones was on TV. And in contrast, Urich's career was taking a proper nosedive.

Urich also felt concerned that he had been jerking off over Cynthia while thinking hateful thoughts about Monty Carn. He wondered if there was some kind of horrendous psychological overlap. (Like: when he had cum, whose face was in the forefront of his thoughts?)

Sheepishly, he walked into the big room and was greeted by a bizarre triumph of electronic sounds from the ropey sound system. He adjusted his suit collar, and wiped flecks of powder from his nose – hoping that people might notice. His plan was to shark around for blondes. Dirty, great big blondes. With blowjob mouths.

That would make him feel less sordid.

After the coke had worn off, Urich found himself looking at his watch, and cursing the night. It had been a disappointment: with little interest from the fairer sex.

He'd also spent the last fifteen minutes avoiding Monty Carn. Because Carn, as history could bear witness, had crushed many a prospective good night – as if it were a sport to him. Carn, the uncouth sod, seemed to relish thc potential of seeing Urich unhappy. But tonight that wasn't going to happen. Urich was going to socialise with the ladies – and, perhaps in the process, make Cynthia a little jealous.

Cynthia, however, was nowhere to be seen. She was in the bar, as far as Urich was aware: being a social butterfly probably, and turning heads in that revealing chiffon blouse and velvet thigh-length skirt.

Urich caught his reflection in a mirror on the wall, and made sure his light-brown hair was side-parted; and questioned whether any women would find him attractive. He glanced at his face and was pleased by it. His features were inoffensive. He had a nice manner about him. He was OK.

A small time later, standing by the cloakroom, someone had approached him.

"I'd like to speak somewhere private with you, now," the stranger said formally. It was a man, and not a woman.

"And you are?"

The man, who did not answer immediately, had a long face, and a strong chin. Although not unpleasant, it was the kind of face that you didn't want to look at for too long. His hair, which was long and grey, had been strangled into a ponytail.

"Never mind that for now," said the stranger, narrowing his eyes, as if the room's lights were too bright. The stranger was wearing beige cords and a suede waistcoat, and was a couple of inches taller than Urich. He stared intensely at Urich as if he were trying to hypnotise him, or extract private thoughts from his mind.

He was standing too close, anyhow.

"If you want to learn about how to progress yourself, my friend, I would join myself at the bar in a while," he said in a gruff, but assured tone of voice. He sounded like some old ham actor in a movie.

Urich said nothing. Instead he looked at him as if he had started tap-dancing. In fact, Urich was beginning to feel creeped out by him.

The stranger took a deep breath, and seemed to look at Urich with dismay. And after shrugging his shoulders, he wandered off, overly conscious of his own travel across the room. And must have sensed he wasn't wanted.

"Who the hell was that idiot?" said Urich.

"It's Sime Hunst, you know that don't you?" said Cynthia, who had just arrived with a glass of white wine in her hand.

Sime Hunst was a modern artist. Someone who'd been talked up by the media for quite a while; and someone who usually shunned the limelight. As Cynthia had pointed out: it was quite unusual for him to socialise.

Urich cursed, and laughed quietly to himself. Thinking about it: he saw that the other man's demeanour made sense. Hunst could afford to be peculiar and 'enigmatic' because he was immensely respected. Whereas Urich – wasn't.

And could Urich be blamed for not knowing who he was? Urich wasn't that familiar with modern art. Though he still knew of Hunst by name. Anyone would. His trademark was 'the violence beneath everything'. Chopped-up animals, and dead butterflies. None of it Urich's cup of tea, but good for business: to be seen talking to him.

"You should still speak to him," said Cynthia, before walking off and leaving him alone, in the lingering company of yet another blunder.

Anyway Urich wasn't so sure. Did he even have the resolve anymore? To be patronised by an egomaniac, and on a Friday night as well.

Still, he began to regret his actions; and couldn't help wondering why someone like Hunst would seek him out in the first place.

A little later Urich cheered up. All was not lost.

Hiding amongst the drunken frontline down at the bar was Hunst – nursing a drink. It was time to *carpe diem*, as his blithering superiors were always saying. Self-consciously, Urich heaved his quite tall frame over to the bar and sidled up to Hunst. He ordered a lager, and stood next to him: thinking of a way to excuse his earlier rudeness.

Hunst glanced over, and pretended not to notice Urich. It seemed like he was sulking, tending to his wounds. Under a strip-light from the bar, Hunst's face looked haggard, older than it did before. Urich was also struck by how this slim middle-aged man actually looked like he imagined a real artist to look: shifty, cranky, and annoying.

"I need you to help me...and perhaps I can help you....to progress yourself," said the artist unexpectedly, overwriting some half-baked idea in Urich's head.

This sounded encouraging. Weird but encouraging.

"I want you to advise me," Hunst continued, addressing Urich's eyes in a full-on stare. He was edging closer again, too close for comfort. "I've written a novel...and I've been doing a little research about the market. Hinds Starkey and Sacks are small, which suits me."

Urich couldn't have hoped for a better response, and thought of ways to impress the strange man.

Except Urich knew little about art, although he knew that there weren't many proper artists anymore. Just pretend ones; or rich kids that saw it as an alternative to working in a bank. And definitely not ones prepared to cut their own ear off in a creative funk, like Van Gogh did.

He looked hard at Hunst and saw that creepy, tortured, slow-burning glow: a look that suggested that he could possibly cleave his own ear off. Or perhaps someone else's.

Something inside him was saying to forget about Hunst.

However, Urich knew he had to play the game to survive. He was drowning and some kind of book deal would be a lifeline. Something to keep him working in the industry, at least.

"So what do you think about my proposition?"

"What's the novel about?"

"It's about how we all do things that we know that we shouldn't. BAD THINGS," said Hunst, tapping his nose. Following this, he took a long sip of lager, with his eyes never leaving Urich's face, and wiped his mouth with the back of his hand. Urich waited for some elucidation. But none came.

"Oh," said Urich, wondering what kind of things Hunst was exactly talking about. "Is it true or fiction?"

Hunst grinned, as if he were pleased that Urich had asked him.

"Aren't they one and the same thing? I find that it is hard sometimes to judge between the two."

Urich wasn't quite sure what Hunst was talking about, and suspected that he was being pretentious. He had actually begun wondering where Carn had got to – though he tried to give Hunst the impression he was definitely still listening. Ironically, he noticed that Hunst had become distracted himself, and saw him move his head to the left, to peer at something. It was Cynthia.

Urich detected Hunst's small eyes delight at the blonde's presence, and this was not good; he'd had taken his eye right off the ball...

"And you are?" asked Hunst.

Cynthia – the Chelsea-born office assistant – was 27 years old, with long banana-blonde hair; and not particularly ambitious. She had ideas and plans, which never seemed to come to fruition. She liked men, and disliked drugs. (Though she kind of liked men who did cocaine as she found that it made them more competitive for her attention.)

Urich expected, in a way, that someone like Hunst would be uncomfortable in the company of Cynthia, and was intrigued to see what would happen. He watched intently as the artist conversed with the blonde; and was aware that there were sparks in their meeting. Not good! He noticed her attentiveness, and those parted lips. Worse still, he continued to watch as she pressed up against Hunst's arm. He saw Cynthia smile coyly, and the artist seem comfortable about her.

In a micro-second, he imagined them naked, sweating and fucking. Cynthia – with her oval face, good advice, and red lips – was for him only?? Urich's soul sneered at their mindlessness, their smiling, their focus on each other. As if only THEY existed in the room.

He watched the artist and Cynthia share another joke and his stomach began to turn. With red-hot concern, he saw her plant a kiss on Hunst's obliging cheek – which was the point at which he stormed off.

Brooding the other side of the bar, Urich thought of ways to make her jealous. A brunette to his left, walked by in a strapless dress, smoking a cigarette. Urich had noticed her looking at him – and was interested. The woman seemed fed up with things, and he waited for her to glance again.....but she never did.

The place was a bore. He had changed his mind about it. Moodily, he left cutting a swathe through the endless lines of blondes and suits. But he stopped. He couldn't leave on such a low? Maybe he should go back in and take home the plain (and approachable) brunette. But he didn't.

Outside, the cold air hit him like a slap in the face.

He wondered what he was doing. Had he lost his mind?

Why was he acting like a lovesick teenager when there was a business opportunity called Sime Hunst in there, on a plate. It was a Godsend – surely.

And what was Urich doing?

He was clearly telling God to fuck off.

It was about 1am and Urich was outside, amid the odour of Hotdogs and the sound of shrill voices. He was sulking, and wanted to hide from the world. But within minutes, he saw Cynthia step onto the empty street, click-clacking in her tall heels. Hunst was there with her, which made him feel on edge.

And then something kind of unnerving happened.

Noticing how they were looking for cabs, Urich – previously standing behind a group of office workers – made himself more visible to them, and stepped into view.

But this was the odd thing.

Urich was sure that Hunst, from a distance, had caught his eye. And then he had thought that Hunst had tapped his nose, suggestively, whilst staring back – as if trying to warn him away. Like he was trying to intimidate. But that was just silly. Hunst couldn't have seen him: he was too far away.

"There you are," said Cynthia, on noticing Urich. She linked arms with him, and Urich smiled idiotically. Then all too quickly: – a taxi pulled up, and Cynthia urged him to get inside. Hunst got in, and Cynthia was left standing on the pavement.

"Where do you live?" asked Hunst, as the cabby tried to start the rickety engine. Urich – choking on aftershave, stale smoke, and air-freshener – saw Cynthia look at him from outside the cab's window.

"What's going on?" said Urich, feeling a little motion sickness as the cab pulled away from the kerb finally. What had happened to Cynthia? Had she merely used the meeting to put in a good word for him? Or had Hunst just got rid of her?

Hunst eventually broke a long silence: "I'm considering that you might be the right person to help me sell my novel."

Urich was complimented by this, despite finding Hunst unlikeable. Moreover, he knew that this man, this subterranean celebrity, could be the ticket that he had been dreaming of. Or maybe not?

What, in fact, did a modern conceptual artist know about writing? Artists didn't read, they just looked – Urich imagined. Or if they did read, it was just the small-print of their fat contracts. Artists used clever slogans, in really short sentences. That was the extent of their relationship with the written word.

"Are you familiar with my work?"

14

Hunst had exploited another silence in the cab, and dropped a bombshell.

"What?" said Urich.

Urich could just see a big blurry mass of work. He couldn't really differentiate between anything. He saw attitude, rebellion and death in a hurried mental collage. But it was all much of a muchness. You see, if he named a work, he couldn't be sure that it was one of Hunst's. And he didn't want to risk mentioning one of Hunst's counterparts; thus offending the obviously highly-strung artist.

"Well?"

Urich, in a vision of the future, saw disappointment in his father's eyes; and now, in the present, he saw an opportunity slip, an opportunity much needed. This was a chance for him to back a winner for once. He needed a biggie. And knew that a book by someone of Hunst's repute would sell.

BUT did Hunst suspect that Urich didn't have the Midas touch anymore? Urich – through his own eyes, in private – was a fuck-up. And why? Because he had passed on some writers. Including a Booker winner. He had been 'unwise' – in industry speak.

"Well, are you familiar or not!"

Urich had been thinking and not saying anything. He thought quickly and desperately. He had to recall Hunst's work. He remembered dead women, bears, sharks, veal (?) He recalled a dismal barbecue scenario and someone swimming.

"Of course I am."

"Good."

Hunst didn't test Urich any further, which was a relief.

The cab hit a couple of speed bumps in quick succession, and Urich heard Hunst cuss to himself. He watched him sneer like the kind of nut you might find on the top-deck of a night bus. Then the cab stopped in a grey, unfriendly street. Hunst passed the taxi driver a fifty through the side window.

"Got anything smaller?" said the driver meekly, as if it were mandatory to say that. "Yes, your cock," said Urich with a broad grin. And realised that it was not a very clever or witty comment to make (and quite confusing as to whom it was directed at: the meek driver or Hunst?) Damn, Urich thought – regretting the endless crudeness and banter of the men's toilets at Hinds Starkey and Sacks.

Hunst crossed the road. Urich followed, mulling over his bad joke – feeling somewhat unwise.

He was lagging behind now.

They were somewhere in South London and Urich began to feel apprehensive again.

Why hadn't Cynthia come with them? Internally, he wrestled with reasons, and was annoyed at her for abandoning him. He didn't trust Hunst, and was worried that his own lack of knowledge about art would be exposed.

"Sit down," said Hunst, after they had entered the flat.

His apartment was minimal and ultra-clean. Teak-obsessed, with marble-topped tables, and some fancy paintings. There was also a big flat-screen TV with accompanying speakers. It was just what Urich liked. The walls were the colour of vanilla ice cream. All the furniture seemed low, near to the floor.

16

They sat on tiny trendy chairs – saying nothing initially, and Urich hoped that Hunst would turn the big TV on. But Hunst, still not saying anything – left the room and went into another, which was lit up by a red light. Within a minute, he returned, smiling – and carrying a metal box. This he placed on a table. Then he said something unsettling, and random.

"You do seem like a good egg," he muttered, opening the lid of the metal box, "but I think you'd be happier if you were just a bit fried."

The artist laughed. And Urich, in response, creased his face up and was about to laugh too, but didn't. Instead, he tried to decipher the artist's statement.

"It's time the fireworks started," said Hunst.

He spoke in a hassled drawl, sounding almost bored – as if he had brought out this same box many times before.

"What's going on?" said Urich, sotto voce.

"There's no need to be secretive now. There are no secrets in here," said Hunst, whilst offering Urich a porcelain pipe, and a lighter.

Urich, without saying a syllable, lit the pipe, and sucked up the acrid smoke. After a short time, Urich's brain exploded with illicit happiness and he became fascinated about having more money, in a quick-time vision of the future.

He sat back in his small chair, and thought about things. About what Hunst stood for. He felt out of his depth being with this artist. This was not a writer but an artist – a much nastier breed, more honest; interested in bodily functions and obsessed with death.

17

Writers were much nicer and had kind polite wives. (Well, according to Urich's own experience of meeting clients from Hinds Starkey and Sacks.)

Urich was wired, and imagined his eyes to look a little wild. He'd never done crack before, and closed his eyes in a moment of toxic bliss.

They were both sitting on small chairs, about a metre apart. And must have looked ridiculous. He looked around at the geometry of the room, and kept re-exploring the fact that the furniture seemed to be near to the floor. He felt at a slant.

He also noticed that Hunst had become less sociable. Like a mood had overtaken him. Soon, he began to feel slightly unwelcome. But necessary…as though Hunst wanted him there for a reason. Urich lit a cigarette and convinced himself not to be bothered about this. He was becoming higher, gradually.

But at peak of this feeling, it got icy. Urich picked up a coldness, a kind of underlying violence in the atmosphere. The type of violence – Urich suddenly thought, quite cleverly – that Hunst was famous for concealing in his work. Urich laughed and caught Hunst's eye.

"What's in this shit?"

"God only knows," said Hunst.

Hunst's voice was unnatural, Urich now observed. 'Artificial' and kind of macabre, and it was freaking him out.

Within the next five minutes or so, Urich groaned. He was conscious of perspiration dotting his face, on his forehead mainly and below his nose. He felt warm. Much too warm.

An indeterminate amount of time had passed.

"Are you alright?" asked a voice.

"What?" said Urich drowning in an overall restlessness.

"I didn't say anything," uttered Hunst.

Urich heard the voice again, telling him to 'just chill out'. He felt, he thought, like he was entering the early stages of an acid trip. Something was not right, and he began to fret about Hunst having slipped him something...

It was a female voice.

"Who's that?" said Urich, squinting, and conscious of grinding his teeth. He turned around, trying to wake himself out of an unexpected delirium.

"Just me?" said a girl, from somewhere in the confines of the flat.

The voice instructed him to come and join her.

Urich knew what was going on: Hunst, in an effort to impress Urich, had hired a prostitute for the occasion. But then Urich considered that maybe this girl-who-he-had-not-even-seen-yet was always there, on a retainer – just hanging about, waiting to fuck his artful friends. *These artists, Christ, they were depraved.*

"Go in the other room and be less up tight," ordered Hunst, and Urich felt even more uncomfortable. He didn't like the 'control' in Hunst's voice.

Shit – Urich thought. His conservative upbringing was tapping him persistently on both shoulders. He could almost hear his mum and dad imploring him to find a more suitable friend. Someone with a proper job.

Urich wiped a hank of hair off his own forehead. He was sweating and worried that his hair was becoming constantly plastered to his cranium. He felt a mess in comparison to Hunst.

What was going on here? Urich was asking himself questions, and got off the sofa, with tension burning in his shoulders. He felt the urge to just walk out; but, immersed in an idea he had just imagined, was compelled to meet the owner of the voice.

"She's in the bedroom," said Hunst, smoking a cigarette, "go on, don't be frightened."

But Urich didn't feel scared. Quite the opposite: he felt strong.

There, lying on a bed in the near-darkness was a girl who could be no older than twenty-two. The light from the hallway informed him of crimped red hair, which was clearly dyed. A closer inspection revealed a nose-ring and pierced eyebrow. (She was the kind of person who Urich would not usually spare a thought; from another world, as far as he was concerned.)

Urich felt unfocused now, and his mind became foolish with some strange thoughts. He sat down on the bed next to her, and glanced at her side-on.

Her perfume, which filled almost half the room, was nice: natural, Body Shop maybe. She had on a white T-shirt and jeans.

He looked at her again and, close-up, considered that she was maybe younger than he had originally thought. All of a sudden, Urich got the fear and felt that he was being set-up.

The girl removed her jeans and stood there in her knickers, and looked very slutty through Urich's drug haze. He saw slim thighs; and dark pubic hair through diaphanous knickers.

"He says I've got to be with you," the girl said, cautiously.

"What?" said Urich.

"He…the man…in there…says that I have to sleep with you, do what ever you want…"

He glanced back into the other room, squinting in the mist of red light coming from Hunst's ceiling. Hunst was gone, maybe in the toilet.

Urich felt a surge of honesty, and became compelled to confide in the young woman. "I have someone I like very much," he said feebly. "So…I don't know about all this."

"Are you fucking her?"

Urich paused and considered the reason why he hadn't and – marvelling at the outline of the girl in the half-darkness, decided to forget about his unconditional love for Cynthia. Just for a while.

"So are you going to go with me, or what? You can do what you like, y'know," the girl said in a, now, distinctly regional accent.

But Urich wasn't ready; his head was all messed up. He needed to make small-talk, to sober himself up; make him function better.

"How old are you," said Urich, in a formal way – wiping the hair from his eyes.

"Twenty-five," the girl said.

"What do you do?"

"What you think!?"

21

"I mean do you have any ambitions?"

"I write, sometimes."

That was the last thing Urich wanted to bloody hear, and became deaf to that side of her.

"What's your name?"

"It's Liz."

She moved away from him and took her necklace off, placing it on a table near the bed. The necklace looked expensive and had a gold locket attached to it.

Urich picked it up in his hand and admired it. One day, he imagined, he would present Cynthia with something like that.

"Nice, isn't it," he said softly, feeling that he was losing his voice.

She turned around and faced him, and said something 'dirty' to him, that made him feel embarrassed. He then grabbed the girl by a clump of her hair and pulled her knickers down with his other hand. He felt invigorated by the 'moment'; however unusual it was.

"Not so rough!" she said, complaining about his intense hurry.

He was unfocused with a lust that he had not recognised in himself before. Then, ravenous, he went to kiss her mouth. He made her step out of her knickers, bent her over the bed and took his hard prick out and entered it into the crease between her arse cheeks. He wanted to fuck her right inside her arse, but could hardly see what he was doing; and, before long, the room was starting to stir, and his vision began to slowly strobe.

And Hunst arrived at the entrance of the bedroom, smiling.
He appeared to be smiling.

CHAPTER TWO

It was about Four O'Clock in the morning, and Urich felt ashamed with himself for what he had done, and needed to speak with Hunst. He went into every room in the house and could find no one.

But was this? A leather briefcase lying on the kitchen table. It was wide open and inside was a manuscript, bound in a thick blue card.

According to a yellow post-it note, it was called "The Confessions". And scribbled in biro on another post-it, was the inscription:

A present for my newest, brightest friend.

Urich grabbed what was rightfully his, and let himself out the flat.

In a cab home to Vincent Terrace, Islington – he held the manuscript in his hands and kissed it. Today, he decided, it would mark a new page in the book of Jonathan Urich's strange old life. This would be the end of career deadlocks and financial strife.

Still wired, he was able to shut his eyes for a minute, to dwell on positive things. But then a thought awakened him from his relaxed state. He was thinking, undeniably, about the girl – and sitting up suddenly, he worried that something was not quite right about the experience.

A few hours later.

The phone rang. And Urich picked up, having only had a few hours sleep. He could hear the person at the other end breathing. Despite the fact that the caller was silent and said nothing, he suspected that it was Hunst.

"I see you have the manuscript, which is good," he eventually said. And didn't mention the girl. "Have you read it, friend?"

Urich's head was throbbing and he was beginning to anticipate some kind of nervous hangover. Of course he hadn't read it; he'd barely looked at it. Was this man mad?

"I'm sure Monty would like it…if you don't want it?"

Cunt – Urich thought.

"Monty's not the way to go."

"Isn't he," said Hunst, sounding tired. "That's very stylish of you, putting down someone from your own firm."

"Sorry, it's just that I feel terrible," said Urich, trying to excuse himself, "I'm still wasted from last night and…I'm just so tired."

Hunst said nothing, letting him get sucked down into the vacuum of the disconcerting silence.

"I want to speak business," said Hunst soberly. Urich felt relief again.

And then they talked for a bit, and while they did so: Urich began to feel suspicious of Hunst's intentions. And felt that a game was being played, as if Hunst was fully conscious of Urich's recent history at Hinds Starkey and Sacks. Which was not that impressive.

Urich felt defeated – so early on too, and began to care a little less than he had.

"I've flicked through the manuscript Sime, and I've got to say that it needs work," Urich said. He began to lie.

In an instant, he knew what he had to do. He needed to make Hunst feel insecure. Feel small. He had to make Hunst need him. Or Hunst would smell Urich's need. His need to reel something big in.

"It is sketchy, rushed. It needs more attention."

"What if I do know what I'm doing?" Hunst countered, his coldness amplified by the direct connection into Urich's earhole. WHAT if I know exactly what I'm doing!!

"You know something," Urich said, forgetting the means to this incredibly important end, "I'm really bemused by the number of celebrities who think they can just turn their hands to writing. They think they can just do it at the drop of a hat."

And Urich realised that if his own voice was a face, it would be wearing a snarl. His fear of Hunst was causing him to be boorish. That old don't-give-a-fuckness was back. But he didn't want it back. Not now.

"Then maybe I'll go elsewhere."

Urich panicked. "What I'm saying is…it may need attention. Attention is something that is always needed."

"Is that your diagnosis?" Hunst whispered.

"It is," Urich said calmly. And, in private, recalled that he had not read a single word.

He had done it. He had actually convinced Hunst that his work was lacking. It was incomplete, but repairable – in the right hands. Urich's hands, of course. This called for a celebration. He ran over to his 'special film' collection and picked out a videotape (not a DVD). He took the tape out of its thin-card cover and threw all his clothes onto a small pile on the floor. Then he looked downwards at the floor and marvelled at the sordid cover of the movie: all ass, tongue-leering and pained expressions. Something clicked in his brain and he had a chilling thought. Why had Hunst made no mention of the night before? Why no mention of the girl he had slept with?

Something had happened back at the flat…. and Hunst, Urich suspected, knew more than he was letting on.

The phone rang again. It was Hunst again – so Urich put him on hold briefly and quickly slung on a dressing gown, knowing that being totally naked would probably lessen his new feeling of dominance over the artist.

"I've had a wonderful idea," said Hunst, "I've been thinking about what you said to me about people thinking they can write purely because they're famous."

Urich put the phone onto speaker mode and slipped the cassette into the video recorder. He would relax as soon as the conversation ended.

"It's complicated," Hunst said.

So Urich pressed eject with his remote. The video cassette would have to wait.

"Sit down and concentrate…I'm going to explain," said Hunst.

Hunst wanted Urich to sell the manuscript for him. But not to just anyone…not to any old inky publisher. Hunst had someone in mind: someone less obvious than your run-of-the mill publishing type. And someone that Monty Carn would never have thought of.

So what was going on?

Hunst – perhaps the most famous modern artist in the country – wanted Jonathan Urich – the agent who had, of late, sold very little – to sell the damn thing to Ernest Zinner. That was Ernest Zinner – art mogul, advertising hotshot, art dealer, romancer of fine women; lover of anything not yet bought by anyone else.

Jonathan Urich was going to 'upgrade himself', and pull off a very original high-profile deal. He was going to sell Hunst's manuscript as a CONCEPTUAL PIECE OF ART. And what was it going to be called? It would be called: THE UNREAD MANUSCRIPT!

And it would be sold to Ernest Zinner under the following condition:

That the manuscript would never be read by anyone (except, of course, by Zinner and Urich).

Urich didn't quite understand art, but he knew that this idea was conceptually fucking brilliant. How clever! To turn it all on its head. To make a commission by making sure a writer's work could never be read by anyone. Brilliant!

As soon as Urich put the phone down, he paced excitedly around his taupe-coloured flat, his head buzzing with his own greatness. Okay, it wasn't quite his idea, but he had pushed Hunst in that direction.

So Urich, with a definite lilt in his step, threw his dressing gown onto the floor and caught the reflection of his handsome self in the mirror. He looked panic-stricken, suddenly, just as he saw his own image, and was confused.

He was going to win, this time – wasn't he?

CHAPTER THREE

Urich opened four letters and became aware that four different institutions – including his own bank, Natwest – wanted money from him, like yesterday. Financially things were not good at all.

He also had another problem: Monty Carn.

Carn had, somehow, been charming Cynthia. They'd met for a drink, apparently, according to Alexander Tramell's reportage.

And Urich had felt like grieving.

The news of Monty Carn and Cynthia meeting after six was an abomination. Why could they not keep it anodyne, congenial? Why not lunch? Why not fucking breakfast!?

(Although breakfast, he thought, might intimate that sex had occurred the night before)

Urich's heart pounded with a combination of annoyance and mild fury. How could Cynthia find such a sorry drinking partner?

You see, Cynthia was rarely in the office these days; and Monty, on the sly, had been getting her to work for him. The competitive bastard! It was hardly paranoid, though, to suspect that Carn was stealing her way from him. Now that had to stop. But that wasn't all that needed to stop. Urich needed to focus, stop thinking about her for a while. Quit the obsession.

He took a pill from the bottle on the living room table, and swallowed it down with a glass of water. Now to focus...

So what did he know about the art mogul Ernest Zinner?

Not that much. But knew that he used to work in advertising, and was into art that was anarchic and fresh. Zinner liked to be associated with the odd baddie, low life, or those with the social perfume of violence (but not the real hardcore rogues).

That was his style, to knock about with edgy types. Not that he was like that himself: he was a rich boy from an extremely privileged background.

On Monday evening, Urich went to Charing Cross and looked at books on conceptual art, modern art and some just about art. Because on Tuesday, he would need to be an expert. Not a lot of time. But enough for Urich to climb this great slushpile called life.

He would need to be seductive and enigmatic. Though he had doubts about his voice: he sounded too nice. Zinner – as he well knew – surrounded himself with oiks, working-class boys, obstreperous little bastards. Some of them: tattooed.

Perhaps, Zinner would be impressed by Urich's no-bullshit way of working – a style that some saw as 'too Hollywood' for the genteel world of publishing. Maybe now, he thought, this approach could finally apply.

He would phone him on Tuesday morning, first thing. And he would sound like the sort of player that buttered Zinner's bread.

But Zinner's phone was engaged on Tuesday morning. And right through much of the afternoon. So he sat back in his chair and asked the office temp Caroline to make him a micro-cup of expresso. And watched her skinny arse sashay out the door after acting on his words. His confidently-expressed words.

And again, something snapped. Recognition. He thought about the previous night and strummed the spikiness of new stubble under his chin. (*What about the girl?*) No. He must focus on the here and now. Not get bogged down in guilt and paranoia. When the secretary arrived with the coffee, he thanked her profusely – and, in private, reprimanded himself for being too polite. He slouched in his chair, feet up on desk. He would wait for a while and call Zinner back. Then he heard the familiar ring of his phone.

It was Hunst again with his usual "caller withheld" number.

There was a while before Urich or Hunst spoke. The pause just went on, and on. And it begged Urich to wonder, who had spoken last.

"I'VE JUST HAD AN IDEA," Hunst said, his voice up an octave, and sounding decidedly more affable.

"Tell me."

"My previous vision is all wrong."

"No it's not. It's wonderful," Urich said, imagining a great opportunity crumble into shit dust.

"The main concept is flawed and I know what is missing with this Unread Manuscript project."

"Go on."

"I'm too successful for the idea to have any soul to it."

"Soul? I don't understand?"

"It would make more sense if we had a struggling artist attached to my manuscript."

"Why?"

"Because…then the struggling writer is selling their soul to the art world for MONEY. But as a trade-off, they are having their writing validated as art."

"No, it should be you as the writer…people will be interested."

"Are you just saying that purely because of my fame?" enquired Hunst.

"No. Absolutely not!"

"Well, I believe, friend, that this is a very stimulating concept we are talking about here…I want people to be charmed by the fact that a nobody is having their work recognised. Which will beg one to ask the question: can writing be considered as art? Especially if no one is allowed to read the work?"

Uh huh – Urich thought. He listened and was alert – but still, he read Hunst's words back in a mental mumble. It all seemed a bit pretentious to him.

"And – fuck! Yes! – I know what else!" Hunst screamed.

"What?" asked Urich, baffled – conscious of Hunst's newly-found sense of normality. The artist had dropped his ice act: like other mortals, he was being 'enthusiastic'.

"The artist, our writer has to sign the contract with Zinner in his or her own BLOOD."

"That bit sounds good," said Urich.

There was another silence on the phone and Urich's mind really began to snake around the subject.

"So what are you thinking?" Hunst asked.

Urich was now thinking about the prostitute from the other night, though he wouldn't admit that to Hunst. Instead, he would just tell him whatever he wanted to hear.

The morning of the next day, Urich awoke to a particularly disturbing dream, which, clearly, had been influenced by his new interest in modern art. It was disgusting and he would keep it to himself.

That same morning, he looked at another book about art. This one was by Burgundy Conews. Conews made art very simple and 'grounded it' as much as you could expect. The book – called *ARTexplained* - made a lot of sense, and mentioned Warhol a few times. Not that anybody talked about Warhol too much these days, as the book said not to.

After drawing up a contract for an existing client, Urich dialled the number sheepishly and crossed the fingers on his left hand. A secretary spoke and recognised Urich's voice. She told him to hold, and then Urich planned incisive things to say to her after she returned…

But it was him! Urich clicked his fingers to snap his brain into action.

"Hello, Mr Zinner!?" said Urich, his heart pounding. His ears were buzzing with nervous excitement. He couldn't speak for what seemed a long time.

"Who the hell is this?

"Jonathan, er... Urich."

"What is it that you want?" said Ernest Zinner, sounding tired in that way that extremely successful people do. He also sounded a lot better-bred than Urich expected.

Then Urich, all of a sudden, didn't know what to say. He had gone blank. But not to worry: he could improvise, freestyle..

Fortunately, in the nick of time, an idea did arrive...

"I want to tell you a good story," he said, trying to affect the manner of Bob Hoskins in one of his earlier films.

Zinner appeared to be unimpressed. Then, briskly, he became quite angry.

"What is your problem Mr Urich?"

"I don't have a, er.....problem," said Urich. "I just have a rather good solution."

"A solution....by God, your manner is...just so uncouth?"

"Like much of your art?" Urich pointed out, in a vicious tenor, trying to imagine that Zinner would respect his hard-line posturing.

"Hurry up and tell me what you phoned to tell me!"

"Right...a film student rings up John Travolta's agent and... requests Travolta to be in a short film. Why would Mr Travolta want to be in your student film? says the agent. Tell him its art, says the student. The agent relays the request to Travolta. Travolta says tell him this: I'm making two Hollywood movies back to back and earning £16 million. With that money I'm going to buy a Picasso. Now that's what I call ART."

"It was Michael Caine."

"No it was a Picasso…"

"No, no…this a well-known story about Michael Caine. It's one of Burgundy Conew's favourite anecdotes. Anyway, why the hell do you think you have the right to talk to me when you don't even know what the hell you are talking about!?"

"I don't know," Urich said. In fact, this was a stupid thing to say, because he did know. At least he thought he did. *(He shouldn't have been drinking, he knew that much.)*

Well, it sounded like a good idea at the time. To be that indifferent to Zinner's majesty. His bloody almighty reputation.

Zinner said nothing, and Urich followed suit. And then Urich, his heart sinking, became disheartened. He thought: what was the fucking point in this little scam? He had obviously come on far too strong – and blown it. So he decided to regale an uppity arseholish Ernest Zinner with the details of his dream from that morning. The explicit details.

"I had a dream last night…"

"Mr Urich…what indeed was your dream. Excite me!"

"I dreamed that I was being fiercely rogered by the art critic Brian Sewell."

"That is an unfortunate dream, and quite disturbing," he said softly with regret on Urich's behalf.

"You're telling me!" said Urich, sighing – and really not caring any more.

"However, it's not uncommon to us recipients of modern art criticism," stated Zinner.

Then laughed. And liked Urich all of a sudden (and probably dismissed Urich's petulant manner as a bit of harmless attitude). So Urich talked more, and the words, in a jumble, fell out of Urich's mouth; but luckily, most of them in the right order.

And he sold Ernest Zinner, hook, line and sinker on Hunst's clever idea.

Urich, as advised, had pitched the idea without Hunst's name attached and highlighted the need to have a struggling writer sell his or her soul to him – in exchange for money; the ultimate prize: £100,000.

Zinner agreed. And said the strangest thing. He asked if he had to read the manuscript. And Urich said "no, of course you don't have to do anything you don't want." And Urich remembered what the art critic said about Zinner in the art book. That Zinner was dyslexic and saw things more in visual terms. Like Steven Spielberg.

Now Urich was left with a problem. He was the one left with the task of finding a struggling artist/writer. Urich laughed at the obvious irony. He had the work of plenty of struggling writers, right there in his slushpile. But that was immaterial. He just wanted a mugshot, a face. A cipher. Someone to represent the plight of the struggling artist.

But who?

And then it came to him:

Cynthia.

For Cynthia had always wanted the limelight. She craved it – first as a model, which didn't quite really work out. And second,

37

as an actress. Which didn't work out either. She was well-off and beautiful alright, but just not successful.

And, of course, she had mentioned that she always had wanted to be a writer!

Urich knew that Cynthia would be very grateful. Oh why mince thoughts?! The blonde would screw the very life out of him for that kind of exposure. And was Urich so shallow to second-guess such gratitude?

Urich knew that his chances of being with Cynthia were limited. And the clock was ticking. She was within reach, he reckoned, as she was (currently) just a secretary – and any modelling work she had done was not so recent. But what if, one day, she became more successful than him after landing some big flash make-up contract? Would he still be able to continue the closeness? Or would she drift?

Urich knew that he had to make an impact on her, like right now.

That was the thing about Urich: he was self-aware unlike social retards like Monty Carn. Urich knew that, yes, he could be shallow. Everyone was to a degree! And then he was humbled, suddenly, by a quite mature understanding of his own limitations.

In celebration of this new sense of humility, Urich decided to have a moderate line of charlie and a one-skin joint of hash. After smoking it, he thought about the prospect of succeeding for a change, and smiled accordingly.

It was time to become ruthless again.

CHAPTER FOUR

Some weeks had passed, and Ernest Zinner had much on his mind.

Tonight the world could preview Ernest Zinner's latest acquisition in the Zinner Arcade, Kensington. It was a palatial space with everything from empty boxes to wall-high Rothko's. There were miniature water-fountains with pink water spurting forth, and ironic paintings of Princess Diana.

"It's all a load of Pollocks," said Marc, his South African banker friend – at nothing in particular. Zinner forced a laugh and regretted his friendship with the dull South African.

Ernest Zinner was dressed for the occasion. In a frilly-sleeved Lord Byron-style shirt, a mauve blazer and sandals – he sped around the venue in a manner that was at odds with his usual ennui. Much, of course, depended on reaction to the 'Unread Manuscript'. If they could accept this – then, commercially, the future was wide open to wonderful possibilities and schemes. Perhaps, this could see him propelled into another league. A place where criticism (which was 'violation' to him) was less common.

"So no one can read it?" questioned his close friend Marc from South Africa. "That's odd."

But what if his dim-wit friend was right? What if it was just "odd" and not 'challenging enough'. Zinner sipped wine in a tiny moment of inertia. Wasn't it obvious? The cultural connotations! Zinner second-guessed what the critics might say. Was this a dull exploitation of audience expectation? Was it overpriced? Did it matter?

He looked around the big room: this pastel, spartan area that had witnessed many a submissive sigh from critics and audience alike. All of what he saw in this big room had confirmed what he had already suspected: he was not the kind to be taken in. It was OK.

10 minutes later.

Behind the all-important main table, the cameramen plodded about and dumped heavy equipment. A couple of industry veterans started lining up shots of the empty glass box, which involved squinting their eyes a lot. The crowds watched the cameramen, and some – the dumb ones – were entranced like children.

Urich was looking smart as usual. He'd combed his glossy light-brown hair into a side-parting; and wore his favourite Italian-cut brown suit (which had a gold lining that he adored).

In contrast, Cynthia had never looked so dowdy in her life. She was wearing sneakers instead of heels; a sweatshirt instead of a low-cut blouse. And her long blonde hair? It was black, carefully-messed and short.

And her lack of self-doubt, her usual sang-froid? – all gone with the exit of the lovely blonde hair, according to Urich's personal theory.

But she was LIZZY now…

Zinner and Urich had already agreed that 'Lizzy' was a much more democratic name; something that people could really relate to. It reflected the struggle of the artist and was easier for simpler people to remember. Yes, Lizzy was a good name.

But there was a problem for Urich to consider. How was he going to explain about the blood? Because, as planned, Cynthia would need to sign the contract in blood. Her own blood. This had been stipulated by Hunst.

13 minutes later.

Urich went outside for a smoke and searched through his navy blazer pockets for a Silk Cut.

"HAVE one of...these," said Carn, placing a cigarette in Urich's mouth. Urich wondered why Carn was here, threatening to rain on his well-deserved parade. Carn's presence was discomfiting and made Urich reluctant to look directly at him.

"Cynthia is...," he said, "being made into a monkey, all because YOU want to climb trees!"

Monty was embarrassingly drunk, as usual, and Urich surveyed his colleague's face, and itched to tell the lurching six-foot rival to shut the hell up. Monty stood there: grinning like a gigantic child; puffing stupidly on a cigarette.

"So Urine, couldn't deal with writing...had to deal with arty farties and their pretty pictures."

"That's right," said Urich, lighting the cigarette.

"Would you like a bit of bacon then, wally?"

"What?"

"To go with the egg that's going to be on your bloody mush?"

Mush!?

Who the hell said things like that anymore? The prick.

Carn slapped Urich on his back and left, after spying a tall blonde on her own.

Urich watched his fat adversary waddle, supposedly dignified, into the distance and approach the blonde. But instead of talking to the blonde – Carn made a beeline for Zinner. Urich was not happy about this and knew that Carn was trying to muscle into his 'action'.

But Carn was wasting his time.

Things were sewn up between him and Zinner.

The rock music (Primal Scream, Elton John, some Texas) formed a sonic wind and blew gently over the muzak of a thousand similar conversations. Waitresses danced around with plates of canapés in their small hands; and the champagne flowed. Everyone from the gallery smiled; many of the guests didn't – as smiling, of course, made people look naïve. Then, too quickly, the music stopped and an audible drone began: as if a swarm of bees had descended on the evening.

Eventually, by word of mouth, attention was drawn to the round white ceramic table in the middle of the room. Seated at the table were Urich, Zinner and Cynthia. Cynthia was clutching the blue-bound manuscript like her life depended on it. And at one point, opened it quickly – to give the photographers evidence that the pages did actually have writing on.

Urich sipped more of his champagne, and glanced over at Cynthia – noticing her nervousness, and how she wasn't used to this kind of exposure. Whilst continuing to study her, he realised how he was fascinated by this unconfident side to her.

Zinner then stood up and clinked two fluted champagne glasses together. Everyone listened. He was about to make a speech.

"YOU are in the presence of newness now…

…the 'same' is our enemy. And there is nothing 'the same' about what is about to happen tonight!"

He reminded guests about how the media liked to vilify him and how he had learned to put up with it. Then he said that by making Lizzy sign a Faustian pact with him – he is "kind of" playing up to the media's view of him and was "sending up his own mythology".

"Faustian what?" said Cynthia loudly, sitting up in her chair.

Urich shushed her and urged her to listen to Zinner's speech.

Zinner admitted that he liked, occasionally, to mess with magazine editors and critics (which Urich thought was a pretty crapulous thing to say if they are there in front of you). But he assured us all that we must get to know him, especially the "beautiful women in the room" – to an uncomfortable ripple of forced laughter.

Then he asked if anyone had any questions.

Someone spoke.

It was a man, to the right, wearing a fedora hat, which obscured much of his face. He was slim and spoke in measured tones. He was well-dressed: in a tailored grey suit with black spotless brogues.

"Lizzy," he said coldly, "what happens if the manuscript is somehow read. Have you thought about the consequences?"

A few people laughed. It was as if the man had confused 'art' with something out of a Dennis Wheatley novel.

"I have considered this and…"

She stopped mid-sentence, and smiled as much as she could: to compensate for not giving a proper, suitable response. The man's question appeared to unsettle her. Amused, the man bowed his head like a cat, and left her to think about this decision. Then others, mainly journalists, asked Zinner about his own take on the quirky artpiece.

Cynthia was clearly shaken by talk of the Faustian pact, and had become awkward and vague. So Urich put his arm around her, sensing her unease; and told her that the second part of the ceremony was due to begin.

And then it did begin.

One of Zinner's corpse-like assistants appeared at the table and offered her palm, face-up, to those seated at the table.

"What's that?" Cynthia said to the small female assistant.

"Something to complete the ceremony," said Zinner casually, referring to a large pin in the hand of the assistant. It looked like something you might find in an embroidery box.

He then told her to smile and "pose lovely" for the photos. While she looked for cameras, he clutched her index finger; and jabbed her finger with the large pin. Blood trickled out of it, and she shrieked. Now Zinner and Urich, in a quickly-established unity, told her what to write – despite her shaking. It was at that moment that she started crying.

When the blood had stopped flowing, they pricked her index finger some more. And Urich, apologising, grabbed hold of Cynthia's shoulders to comfort her. The audience wondered what the hell was going on – but enjoyed the drama nonetheless.

Still crying, she wrote – with blood dripping from her finger – on the brown parchment-like scroll. This took longer than expected and, before long, the scroll became red and messy with her scribble.

She wrote (if one could call it that):

I, Lizzy Jones, sell this novel to be kept in a glass box, unread, for all eternity.

At once, the crowd began clapping, and might even have given Lizzy, Urich and Zinner a standing ovation – had they not been standing already. But Cynthia was still upset, and ran off to a loo – keen to disguise her tears.

Zinner and Urich, in contrast, were as contented and relaxed as well-fed cats; and, in a sunny mood, Zinner explained more about 'the artwork' with a variety of journalists: and told, for example, how the struggling artist Lizzy was to receive her payment of £100,000 pounds.

Except, in truth, the money (or most of it) was earmarked for Hunst and some for Urich. Cynthia was, in effect, only employed as an actress. (Still, another dream had come true for the struggling model.)

In the cab home, Urich imagined being in the pages of OK magazine, and dreamed about a high-brow TV show, with someone like Clive James asking him and Hunst lots of questions.

And that made him think: Hunst, where the hell had he been all night?

That was something that unsettled Urich, as he mulled it over in his drunken mind: swallowing yet another tablet.

CHAPTER FIVE

What a bloody shady business this all was – thought Urich.

Did Hunst have to make everything so suspect? Why did artists have to be so complex?

Urich, as directed by Hunst, took the money – in cash, in a black leather briefcase – to a charity shop in Victoria. He was required to be there for Ten in the morning, and he was told to give it to a young man called Mark.

Urich was required to ask no further questions.

A man – in his mid-twenties, who had exceptionally bad teeth and greasy hair – came out to greet Urich. This was funny, thought Urich. Of all the people Hunst could have used…why such an awkward, gangly student-type? And why in a charity shop?

Urich was uncomfortable with all this; but seeing as Mark was behaving professionally, Urich decided to shelve his doubts.

Urich handed over the black leather case, which contained Hunst's money.

Mark, carrying the briefcase, went into the back room; and returned to the front of the shop, without it. They shook hands eventually; and Urich – unsure what to say to Mark, on leaving – said: "hope to see you again".

But he knew that he most probably wouldn't.

As he walked down the Wilton Road, still stoned from an earlier joint, he briefly wondered if he had been stupid. Too trusting. It was the same persistent worry from a while earlier. But something about the day – its niceness and beauty – made him resist the urge to question his actions.

He had completed another task, satisfactorily.

They were in more papers and magazines than Urich could have hoped for. And some that made little odds to him (such as the wilfully obscure Art Of Focus).

All of this had made Urich start the day with a feeling of tremendous self-satisfaction, and he felt that things could only get better. However, there were the cynics. Many thought that the whole media spectacle reflected rather badly on the incredibly rich Mr Zinner. They felt it was 'merely' an incredibly-original exercise in PR, and not much else.

But Urich swept all that aside, as he re-read headlines such as: 'Lizzy Rocks!' and 'The Pen Is Mightier Than The Brush!' and 'Dead Sharks Give Way To Unseen Masterpiece!'

Art critic Brian Sewell thought that, for him, 'the parsnip had remained pretty much unbuttered'. But did that mean that Sewell liked it or not? – wondered Urich, his mind excited by the flurry of press attention.

Today, he realised, they had become far more famous than any particular day preceding. And that was important to him.

Eventually tired of reading about himself, he put the papers to one side and, reclining on the sofa, tried to imagine being in Hello

magazine (which made him think of having sex with Princess Diana
– inexplicably). After smoking some homegrown skunk, he then
decided to switch the radio onto LBC and heard ordinary people
with ordinary jobs talking about this phenomenon known as 'Lizzy'.
Strangely, somehow, he felt unease at strangers taking about Lizzy.
They didn't know her. Whereas he did.

Hunst would be pleased. Urich had done everything expected
of him, although there was more to discuss. Much more. Urich had
already thought of an encore. Something to excite the cognoscenti,
the critics, and the rest of the world.

So Urich got in touch with Hunst's gallery, *The Black Arts*,
and asked for Hunst's number – which a secretary had vehemently
denied him.

"I have been speaking with Hunst already, lots" said Urich,
irritated at the shrill resistance.

"So why do you, Sir, not have his personal number?"

Urich thought hard. It was a good question.

"Because…he always called me?"

Still, the secretary would not relent. So Urich turned on the
charm for a few minutes until she warmed to him, and gave him what
he wanted.

He phoned Hunst and a loutish voice answered.

"Sime," said Urich.

"Who is this?" demanded Hunst.

"Who is this?"

"Yes, who is this?"

"It's Jonathan. You must have seen the news."

"About what?"

"About us?

"Us? Who the fuck are you?!"

"But I've been talking to you."

"Er, no, don't think so."

"…I've been round to your apartment. Don't you remember we met and were drinking together in the club…?"

"I don't drink anymore, mate."

"But we were talking…about the manuscript, planning all this."

"Not to me you weren't. Someone's been winding you up."

And this begged Urich to ask himself the very pertinent question. Which was: if this knob was really Hunst, then who the bloody fuck had Jonathan Urich been talking to during the last week?

Someone – some shrewd bastard – had been messing with him. That much was clear.

PART 2

CHAPTER SIX

In the darkness, the phone rang and THE THIEF received instructions. He was already awake and had been anticipating the call for a while.

His employer was a man of few words and had ended the conversation within minutes. The heist would be in two days, but first he would need to buy the appropriate equipment.

This would be no ordinary job – predicted The Thief.

CHAPTER SEVEN

Here the manuscript was.

In Zinner's Gallery: The Zinner Arcade, Kensington.

Under lock and key. Inside perspex.

Unread by man, woman or beast.

Only one person had any idea of the secrets it did keep.

The true writer of the manuscript.

CHAPTER EIGHT

The Thief was careful not to drag his axe along the floor. He had hidden himself in the basement below the Zinner Gallery in Kensington; and had been there since the gallery closed. And now he had waited long enough.

It was time to emerge from the shadows and do what he got paid for. In near-darkness, he climbed the stairs; and after unlocking a door with a forged key, entered the main hall of the Zinner Arcade.

He was wearing both nylon tights and a gasmask, in order to hide his identity. The gas mask was, perhaps, a precaution too far – (suggested by his employer, but who was he to argue?)

He walked slowly, a step at a time, up the stairs toward the main gallery – clutching the axe. Beneath his excessive disguise, his breathing was difficult and he felt stifled. But the show had to go on.

He growled inside his mask, and persevered.

Within minutes, he was on the mezzanine floor, not far from the room that housed THE UNREAD MANUSCRIPT. He became excited knowing that he would be able to read those pages, those private words for himself.

Of course, he knew that he would not have been the first to have read it. Others like Zinner and Urich would have secured that honour. But it didn't matter.

Nor did the rumours of what would happen if the manuscript was ever read.

And what were the rumours?

The Thief had read the articles, seen the news. And heard the endless cranky theories about this strange new artwork. Not pictures, but words. But what was so special about these words?

Some thought that the text was an astrological charting of the whereabouts of the second messiah. Some thought it a salacious expose of the sex lives of political players throughout the Western world. Others thought it a nonsensical compendium of words. But some – who claimed to know – thought this manuscript to be an amateur affair; with loose ends, relationships that didn't add up, unlikely behaviour and all the blunders and mistakes of an early draft. The Thief would find out soon enough.

He heard footsteps. (The ones that he had been anticipating for the last few days.)

"What are you doing in here!?" asked the grey-haired security guard. He spoke from a distance, while shining a torch in The Thief's direction. He was shaken, definitely. What scared him even more, however, was seeing The Thief calmly pull out a small canister of 'laughing' gas and throw it near his boots.

After the canister leaked its pungent contents into the atmosphere, the guard covered his mouth with his hands. Then, groaning horridly, he collapsed on the floor. And did not laugh.

Still no alarm went off.

The Thief walked into the rotunda and laid his eyes upon the most famous art exhibit in the country. It was in its impressive glass box and ornate metal casing. Next to the manuscript was the contract written in Lizzy's blood.

The Thief, looking quite ghastly, lifted the axe and began smashing the glass to pieces. And still no alarm.

Jesus, Zinner was lax – The Thief thought. Did he actually want people to steal it, or something?

With gloved hands he brushed all the shards and flecks of glass away, until he saw a wide enough gap to pull the manuscript out of. He put the manuscript into a small rucksack on his back, removed his disguise, and climbed out a window in Zinner's office. The window lead to a wide ledge, which lead to a wall. Eventually, the wall lead to a pavement on which he walked, unhurried.

Due to The Thief's skill and courage, one lucky man would be the proud owner of the most talked-about modern artwork this year. One that the rest of the world had only really glimpsed.

And this success, The Thief guessed, might come at a price.

But a price that someone else would pay.

CHAPTER NINE

Zinner entered the gallery and was alarmed by the fact that no alarm actually did go off when it should have. He wanted some answers from his security manager and he would not accept the usual excuses.

He looked around and thought how dull and terrifying his gallery was with the lights off – this place. His place.

He saw the security guard – familiar by face, but not name – and was a touch sad at seeing someone dead. Then the thought occurred to him to leave the guard there; to give him a better purpose in life. He even thought of a title, one that would fit in with other works inside the gallery: *Man dead in the pursuit of keeping art out of the hands of….*

…out of the hands of whom? – Zinner was unsure.

In the rotunda, Zinner was offended and distressed. Or a cross between the two.

"For damn's sake, I only had it for a few days!" he said out loud, itching a non-existent scratch beneath his hair.

Three assistants followed him into the rotunda and watched him with sad, frightened faces.

"Was it forced entry?" One of the assistants asked; and Zinner, shuddering, did not respond.

58

"Nobody must know that the manuscript has gone," he said with a small, frightened voice. Zinner and Hillary both realised the whole point of the art piece had been ruined. Made conceptually redundant.

"Oh damn it," he said to himself, with an authentic sorrow, his face as grey as his hair. "What a load of bollocks," he added, and then kicked a metal bin in a particularly lethargic manner.

Even the rain couldn't ruin the astoundingly excellent atmosphere at Hinds Starkey and Sacks. In Meeting Room 1, Urich, who couldn't bear to look at Monty Carn's insipid face, was being viewed in an altogether newer and better light. Hinds Starkey and Sacks saw him clearly as the "the golden boy" and their only complaint had been not mentioning the company name "just a tad more". All of them, enriched by Urich's success, struggled to come up with an even better idea themselves. But couldn't.

Urich was happy and childishly unfocused. He watched the rain splash against the windows and sat and drank coffee. Occasionally, he drummed his fingers on the edge of the oak table. His eyes were smiling with pride; gleaming bright blue.

He was happy and so were they. In fact, no one could erase the shit-eating grins from their faces. Except for Monty Carn, who sat there uncomprehending, distanced.

"You take the biscuit," said Hinds, chortling through a mouthful of cigar smoke. Urich was flattered and went to take another biscuit from the magnificent plate of Belgian treats.

"I mean… you have surpassed all of our expectations. You've done us all proud," someone said.

Then Urich noticed Monty Carn's face come to life; and worried that: in Carn's small brain, a good idea might have evolved. But fuck that, Urich thought, knowing it was he who had all the clever ideas from now on.

The art bug was contagious, of course, and now the partners wanted Urich to get involved with some pretty way out things. Hinds, the old codger – with the double chin, and listless voice – suggested Urich sell his grandma to Zinner. Just so people would say something like: 'that Urich, he would, could and did sell his grandma'.

But both Urich's grandmothers were really dead, and, besides, Urich thought it a dull idea. Not that he told Hinds that.

At home The Thief read the first chapter and was sickened. How could this girl, this Lizzy, write like this? It was disgraceful, sickening.

It was not right.

After the three chapters, The Thief felt nauseous. It was like someone, in a stream of consciousness, had just written down everything they could about a life of contemptible sadism. There were instances of sodomy and necrophilia…cannibalism. It was like someone was pleading guilty to some things that they just couldn't contain any longer.

It then becomes clear.

This is not written by Lizzy.

This is some satanic exercise; something that has been compiled by some very sick person, or people. In one part of the manuscript, a couple of men torture a woman in a scenario of unquestionable realism.

The Thief flicked through the text. He saw addresses, real-sounding addresses. Like they really might exist. On the edges of some pages were chicken-scratch drawings, done in ink, that could hardly be seen. But they were, undeniably, of something despicable: dismembering, sexual things, not nice.

At Four in the morning, he saw a pattern.

Each chapter is a supposed murder and at the end of each chapter is an address. The addresses are, supposedly, where the bodies are hidden – The Thief thinks.

So what does this all mean? The Thief was confused.

Then he flicked through another chapter and noticed that an anonymous agent had been mentioned several times. The Thief knew that Jonathan Urich was the agent who pulled the deal together. That had been publicised.

But was this despicable text referring to him?

The Thief read on, carefully.

In one instance, on page 45 of the manuscript, Urich is mentioned by name. It talks about an incident with a prostitute. Urich – according to the text – has had sex with a prostitute against her will. He has beaten her senseless. He has put objects inside her. Cut her face up with a sharp knife. Made her scream until she vomited. On page 46, it talks of her screaming and him laughing at her while she is going blue in the face.

The Thief was upset. What if there was some kind of truth to what was written down here? What if it was non-fiction? What if this was REAL?

He made a phone call to his employer and was told to re-read page 23....

In Warren Street, Urich considered having a cigarette, but stopped. He was smoking too much. He would stop the habit altogether but he felt that the occasional few helped strengthen his lungs against infection. God, he thought how dumb he could be sometimes. But didn't mind. Urich knew that being dumb sometimes was preferable to being evil.

But wasn't he evil besides?

What a question to ask yourself? What a question!

Just what was it that he wanted from life? – was another, more suitable question to put to himself. The easy answer to that was: Cynthia.

He wanted Cynthia so much.

He thought of her in French lingerie and imagined the taste of her skin. How amazing it could be, he dreamed, to be able to tell people that he and her were going out – or more importantly: had had sex. No adolescent gropes, or prudish foreplay. Real fucking. And sexual athletics with her in her sexy Manolo Blahniks. In fact, it wouldn't matter if she were wearing Converse or even an old bearded-man's smelly hiking boots. As long as he got to fuck her for longer than a minute.

He began to think about how he even got into this strange business: of books and reading. And how did he? He couldn't quite remember. And then he did: it was his mother had suggested contacting a friend of her best friend; and also, there was his friend Sebby. Sebby's brother was a literary type who had told him about "the long lunches", "the fit women" and "the coke". Urich thought about his mild dyslexia and how no one had hardly noticed. And then he got bored thinking of the past.

He walked down the road, looking in shop windows, and saw them.

Them: Cynthia and Monty Carn. For it was Monty Carn. This was no mirage, no illusion. There he was: all broad-shouldered, round-shouldered, stupid-fucking-shouldered. With his trademark smirk, bad-fitting brown suit, square-toed black shoes, bow legs and prematurely-greying eyebrows. He looked like someone's fucking parent from the 50's (even though he was much younger).

Cynthia seemed caught out – stunned. The pair of them – in vicious synchronicity – seemed as thick as thieves. Urich felt the weight of melancholy on his shoulders. It was a horrible feeling. And to top it all, Cynthia – wearing little make up – appeared more angelic and ravishing than ever.

She took her hand out of Monty Carn's. With apparent guilt.

Carn was the first to speak, and, simpering, said something like, "hello there Urine. Don't you have work to do? People to impress?"

Or something equally mundane. It was hard to be sure exactly what was said, as Urich, immune to Carn's pointless noise, became flustered by how little Cynthia had to say to him – despite their recent adventure.

The whole chance meeting had been awkward, but more than that: it had been regretful.

Urich left soon after, feeling a hollowness, an emptiness that a cigarette could not, would not fix. How could this be? How could he lose to Carn now, after all he had done to ensure winning?

He would get drunk by himself and chain-smoke all night.

The Thief – following specific orders – arrived at Highgate Woods and followed the directions, which were ambitiously detailed. The manuscript said that 'it' was buried in a shallow-ish grave, near the giant Oak tree by the bunker. The one with the engraving of a dragon by its base.

He drove there in his red Nissan, with a shovel in the car's boot.

It was eight in the morning with not too many people around. A few kids, some dog-walkers. No one stuck about for long. No suspicion.

Then he saw something, as he smelled the burning of wood, from way into the distance. He saw it. The cross made out of tree bark – all make-shift. Unprofessional. Hurried.

It had been described in the Manuscript.

The Thief started shovelling and still no one was around. For half-an hour, he got stuck into the damp earth, and smelled autumn. It was windy, and fresh. Then the shovel hit something deep in the ground. The Thief had located a heavy-duty black bin-liner full of something, and hoisted it out of the earth.

The strong bag was tightly-tied with string and thick brown masking tape. With a knife he opened the bag and the smell was getting into his nose, eyes and throat – making him dry-heave, until he was throwing up.

There it was.

This is somewhat past its sell-by date, he thought, recalling the smell of offal: all rancid, pungent. But this is a hundred times worse.

A body had been cut up into bits. That much was clear.

The Thief put a handkerchief to his nose and over his mouth, as he sifted through some putrid intestines, bloody entrails and saw that there was a necklace. It had a locket attached to it.

The Thief wondered how unfair life could be. He grimaced, and spat in disgust. This was the aftermath of some poor bastard's life. This was someone's son, someone's daughter. It was hard, nonetheless, to determine the victim's gender while being that elbow-deep in their guts. (Though, admittedly, the necklace was a dead giveaway.)

Then something occurred to him.

How does his employer know so much?

He has a reason to suspect that his employer is on the side of 'good'. However, The Thief, being a thief, has taught himself never to trust anyone.

He is not, if he is being honest with himself, sure about the intentions of his employer. If he is to be entirely honest with himself: his employer scares the hell out of him.

CHAPTER TEN

The killer had something to say about the fact that the terms of Cynthia's agreement had been broken. He was also marginally disappointed that everyone else was enjoying the limelight, bathing in the magnificent heat of their fifteen minutes.

His fifteen minutes, really.

Primarily, Carpov was the actual core, the crux, the seed of all this self-congratulation. It was all because of him, wasn't it?

Still, he had acquired some money from this silly game that these amateurs seemed to be clinging on to. And in cash, too – so he couldn't complain too much.

But he would have to wait a little longer for the really big payback. And why? Because he was too good at what he did: killing. And when killing was to be done, the limelight was anathema to him. Privacy and space were king and queen to him, then.

But soon enough, they would all want to know about Andrei.

Andrei James Carpov.

Andrei the master of disguise!

Andrei the writer of fin-de-siècle novels!

Andrei the matchmaker!

But most, important of all, Andrei the murderer!

Andrei was surprised that people never stopped to wonder what kind of hobbies or interests killers might have, aside from killing. Andrei liked to read. Avidly. No one really thought of nasty killers doing much else besides killing. Like they were obsessed with it. Yes and no – thought Andrei.

Yes, he had been obsessed by killing. But no, he could not and would not want to do it all the time, even if he was able to. Then it would become commonplace, ordinary.

Andrei had other interests too. For one, he had written a children's book. Even though, the agents and publishers had rejected it, he still thought it worthy of much supermost praise. What did they know, "the hurters"? They said that it was "far too violent", and "off-putting", and "repulsive in a way that frightening fairytales needn't be".

"Stench of Bear" was something that would sit in his drawer for a little longer, sadly; and those who had rejected it would slit their throats in some beautiful synchronicity. Oh, how they would pay in their own blood.

They thought it too "relentless"…

Had they not read the Brothers Grimm? That scared the brown-shit out of the young child Andrei – for certain. Oh, Andrei thought about these people he called "the Hitlerised shit merchants" or the "shitlerised hit merchants". They had hurt him bad. He had taken an axe to many a skull, but their brand of hurt was worse – thought Andrei. Much worse.

They were average bears! Average fucking bears!!

After a while of sharpening one of his many knives, with his electronic knife-sharpening machine (purchased over the TV from some channel or other), Andrei left the pristine kitchen and sat on an armchair and wondered what he should do next.

"What shall I do next?" he said, teasing himself, as he knew exactly what he was to do next.

He picked up the phone and dialled Urich's mobile phone number. It was on answering machine. This angered him.

"Leave a message," said Urich's slimy, treacle-coated smarm voice.

He began speaking, almost without thinking or planning. His voice was wobbly at first, but he managed to keep it together. He wondered if he should conduct his speech in Russian, but decided not to.

Instead, he explained his thoughts on the recent past, after the cue of the beep:

"I want you to choose what happens to your pretty friend. She gave her word in blood and now look what has happened…the contract has been broken…the text has been read…"

He put his receiver down.

Andrei pondered a moment and tried to console himself on his most recent course of action. That wasn't a good idea – he thought to himself – leaving the message, with his own real voice on. What a stupid shitmind – he thought.

Am I becoming like them!?

On the Thursday, at work, Urich received a phonecall from Ernest Zinner. Zinner was nervous and overformal in his language; and his mind was focused on something else. But he told Urich about the break-in at the gallery.

Urich let his mind wander, and considered the possibilities. He remembered Hunst, in his weirdness, saying something about how no one should ever read the thing again, and how it was not a game...and how it must all be taken seriously.

In a flash, he thought about the blood contract that he'd made Cynthia sign. A BREAK-IN? Someone had the manuscript in their grasp and could read it now...

Urich contemplated what this all meant:-

And what exactly did it mean? Did it mean nothing? Or did it suggest: bad luck, spells being cast, witchcraft even?

Was he right to be worried?

Urich felt overwhelmed. How could one man be burdened by so much that he didn't understand? And yet, there was more to concern him: the problem of the Hunst impersonator, and also the problem of Monty Carn.

A shimmer of anxiety tickled his back and neck, and he yearned for some coke – to help him, hopefully, bring clarity to his muddled thoughts.

In the flat with the ice-cream coloured walls, Andrei Carpov sat silently, in the lotus position. He was on the floor of the kitchen, by the gas cooker. He closed his eyes and his head swam in an ocean of premonition. He foresaw obedience on Urich's part. He forecast terror and he predicted a lose-lose situation on behalf of that brattish whore, that symbol of struggle. How dare she represent fight! What does she know about hardship?

He saw shame in a vision so genuine…so made flesh, that he nearly blacked out, lost consciousness.

He ran to his computer and clicked on the email symbol on his desktop. It was time to up the ante: show them that he meant business.

He typed a message, with clammy thin fingers dancing upon the appropriate keys, and tapped nervously on the mouse….

Urich, you are to kill Cynthia …or I am to kill you.

Or if you find that a little severe, then you are to take her against her will.

I will be there with you, watching, maybe or maybe not. And you know how I like to be entertained…

O my friend, it is Rape or the grave?

Take her or I'll remove you from this world!!…

He pressed send. With a decisive pounding on the mouse button, clicking repeatedly.

At 8pm, 2 days later.

Urich stood outside Warren Street Station and thought about a hundred things at once. The food smells made him feel queasy and he lit a cigarette. He thought some more about how he had unalterably changed in the last few weeks.

With a heavy heart, he made a decision. He knew what he must do. He must be bold, force himself to do what he had to. Cynthia would understand, he kept telling himself.

He was sick in a backstreet, next to some rubbish bins.

Cynthia would understand about what he needed to do.

Cynthia had agreed to meet him at a bar in Charlotte Street, called 'Crazy Hare'. There, he decided to play his cards close to his chest and would pretend that nothing much had happened since the big night at Zinner's Gallery.

When she arrived, she was in good spirits – unfazed by her numerous interviews, and fresh-faced. Her hair had been re-peroxided, and she was wearing a black dress, a flash chiffon scarf and open-toed shoes with kitten heels. She looked beautiful for certain, but Urich was troubled. How was he going to break the news to her? How could he?

He would save that all till later. Perhaps, he should broach the equally pressing subject of laughing boy, Monty Carn. He wondered what to say, and saw Carn's infuriating smile in his mind's eye.

"I really think that your spending too much time with Monty…" he said. "…I just think that Carn doesn't have your best interests at heart. He's not on OUR team, you know what I'm saying?"

Cynthia appeared not to be impressed.

"I don't want to speak about Monty right now," said Cynthia, and Urich agreed (with himself) to honour her wishes. Even though he had plenty to say on the subject.

"Ok, I have other subjects," said Urich.

He lit a cigarette and glanced around at all the media types in the swish bar. There was a silence while he tried to think of something less negative to say. But he couldn't think of anything, immediately.

Cynthia spoke, more or less, about the big night. It had gotten too her. She seemed to see the down side of everything. She told Urich about how The London Review Of Books wanted to interview her (or 'Lizzy'), but she had declined because she felt like a fraud. She said that she wanted to be famous for something that she had actually achieved herself.

"Cynthia…you're famous…. and in all sorts of magazines. You know, it's not a crime to be proud of yourself."

"But for what? I am not even allowed to discuss the contents of the manuscript?"

She said nothing more. And then she became ominous.

"I mean what if someone did read the manuscript…what would happen then? I mean where does this thing end?"

She kept referring to the blood signature. She even mentioned how Monty had warned her about it.

Urich did not answer and kept her off the subject of 'consequences'. He was here to make her understand about him. Consequences were off limits for the time being.

(And Monty should have kept his mouth shut).

73

A bumpy taxi ride gave him excuse to be extra tactile with Cynthia. He needed to make her realise his worth. He would turn on a charm offensive.

An offensive charm?

It had become apparent that Cynthia was already tipsy (mainly from rum-based cocktails), and her cut-glass accent had become much sharper than usual. Abrasive perhaps. (He put that down to the stress of being famous). She was acerbic about a variety of subjects: the shallow bimbos who worked at Hinds Starkey and Sacks; "dickheads" like Robson and "that bloody idiot Jerome". Plus dirty, spotty teenagers who apparently looked her up and down on every street corner, "mentally undressing her!"

"They probably wanted to make love to you there and then," said Urich.

There was a silence and Cynthia's nose twitched, as if she disapproved of Urich. Cynthia, it seemed, wasn't being her usual self: the funny sexy person that Urich once knew. Instead, she was acting all subdued, hesitant. It was like her personality was undergoing some alteration. She was trying to be........intelligent.

She started discussing female writers like Siri Hustvedt, who she claimed was Paul Auster's wife. Her wish, she admitted, was to represent someone amazing like Penny Vincinczi or Joanna Trollope – and gushed about the industry, and new writers.

Urich, noticing the change in her mood, tried to become a little less seedy.

It was imperative that he appear more learned.

"Did you know that Saul Bellow's agent once described his testicles as being like jewels," said Urich, in an effort to subtly construct a more sassy ambience. He continued, observing her full attention: "If I ever described one of my clients in that way, I would be fired, probably."

"Jonathan, I'll think you'll find the agent in question was a woman...and they were actually lovers! And you do know that Saul Bellow isn't alive anymore? Besides, who's heard of any of your clients?"

Cynthia was right, as usual. Saul Bellow was dead and nobody had ever heard of the writers that Urich represented (with maybe the exception of other literary agents).

"Did you like Bellow, Jonathan?"

"Yes, he was one of my favourite writers," said Urich; and thought about this assertion and remembered that, in truth, he'd only read one-quarter of *Herzog* and thirty pages of *Seize The Day*. In fact, he regretted ever suspecting that the subject of Bellow (and his wrinkled old nuts) would be a suitable aphrodisiac.

When the conversation on literature had run its course, Cynthia spoke of Monty Carn's new suit; and something within Urich died.

Urich was clearly dissatisfied with the subject matter; and his thoughts trailed off. (And, at that moment, he wondered how many people in the bar recognised him from the recent publicity.)

"What is your problem with Monty? I know you are rivals sort of, but I wish you'd just kiss and make-up."

Urich said nothing and his mouth tightened.

"Anyway, I really love his new suit," Cynthia said, and her mind was somewhere other than in the cab with Urich.

Urich raised an eyebrow and wanted to be sick. He was disappointed with Cynthia's naivety. Didn't she know that when you hate a man, you hate his dog, shoes, suit and anything else he owns? It was a simple rule of thumb.

In any case, Monty Carn's new suit was obviously going to be rubbish. People like Carn didn't wear good suits, in the same way that monks didn't have good haircuts, or down syndrome girls never became supermodels. It was just something that wouldn't happen.

"Monty likes you, you know. He just thinks you're not very self-aware."

That was it. Urich was aware that he could be shallow; but Monty Carn, that smirking fool was sadness incarnate. He was the sort of tawdry drip that one bullied at school. He was the sort of suck-up that told on you if you were smoking behind the bikesheds. He was the sort of prick who deserved to have his innards cut out as if he were a dog.

Urich's face must have reddened and he worried that his thoughts were all becoming a little tumultuous. Soon his forehead felt hot, like you could fry an egg on it.

Eventually, the cab arrived outside his Islington flat and he decided to take things easy. Not to pounce, was his internal dictat. He was to behave, initially.

Once in the living room, he made a beeline for the drinks cabinet and poured out a small vodka with grapefruit juice.

Cynthia was a little red-faced, but still lively.

"Jonathan, no alcohol," she said, spoiling Urich's mood a touch.

But she drank it – after seeing Urich raise an eyebrow, as if to highlight her priggishness.

"Are you…going to disappoint?" she said, slurring her speech, and slouching unimpressively in his leather armchair. She drew her knees into her, so they touched her chin. She giggled.

"Why did you say that?" he said, now curious.

She smiled at Urich's unease and appeared to caress her own mouth, suggestively.

She didn't answer, and asked him another question: "How long am I going to be this bloody owner of this …unread novel?" she sounded harsh, overwrought. Like she was tiring of all this.

"I don't know. As long as you like?" he said, wondering what she had meant about 'going to disappoint'. He was worried that she was beginning not to trust him, after he had fought so hard to appear trustworthy. Her earlier question had thrown him, agitated him. He stopped his train of paranoid thought. Derailed it.

"Is anything wrong?" he asked.

"Oh…I'm just tired. It's hard being a superstar, you know."

She stretched her arms up to the lilac ceiling, and saw that it was out of reach. "Maybe I should become a recluse…"

Urich put his glass to his mouth to take a sip of his drink.

"Why are you looking so serious?" she said, with her arms hanging down by her sides. Urich's face was somewhat severe – acute with something that may or may not have crossed his mind.

"Er, no reason," he said vaguely, and turned from her: slightly embarrassed.

Urich was thinking that – whilst drunk – Cynthia's beauty seemed less remarkable than it had done. Cynthia was lovely and all – with her new fire-yellow scrambled-egg hair, and keen smile. But…?

There was, he deduced, a subtle, barely-detectable unpleasantness to her face.

She looked cruel. That was it. But then he remembered her sense of humour and self-effacing pranks, her empathy; and how she loved children, and how they always seemed to love her. Everyone liked good old Cynthia Price Dennings. Cynthia was hard to dislike.

For a short time, internally, he was confused about his loyalty towards her.

He looked at her and remembered what an odd couple they really were. They'd never ever had sex together. However, one time, last year, around Christmas – they had taken MDMA powder and slept in a bed together. And they had masturbated. But they did this by looking up at the ceiling, in leisurely bliss – without even noticing one another. Urich remembered that the whole ignominious experience was surprisingly unsexual. But at other times, Urich knew and was so certain, that there was something deep down – so inevitable, so tangible – waiting to embroil them both. Some unspent passion, some naked emotion that needed to be recognised. Though this intimacy was always hidden, always clothed by their continual friendship. At the office.

"I'm fed up with being bossed around…I'm going to do just…whatever I want."

Cynthia was speaking in her 'disobedient' voice, suddenly. This made Urich feel excited, especially as he caught her looking at him. She wanted to show him gratitude, Urich reckoned. And why not? He had made her more famous than she could ever imagine.

"I think we should stay up...and party," said Urich and pulled her out of his leather armchair.

She resisted.

"I need my beauty sleep darling?" she said, grinning.

"You're beautiful already," he said. "You don't need sleep... we have to talk."

"Jonathan, sweetness, why don't you shut up and just let me crash out."

But Urich knew he had to keep her up.

For what he was about to do.

"You can't sleep in here," he said, watching her like a hawk.

Stumbling alongside her, he lead her into his bedroom and took his drink with him. She collapsed, laughing, onto his double bed.

He watched her stand up, stretch and – so beautifully chaotic – pull her dress way above her head as if she were suddenly allergic to the fabric. And then he noticed that she had taken it right off and set it on the floor beside the bed. She got into bed and Urich noticed that on the other side of the bed lay her brassiere and lace knickers.

"What... are you...doing... Jonathan?" Cynthia said, slowly, as if she had forgotten how words should follow one another.

Urich, in a hurry, was taking his clothes off.

After having turned off the bedside lamp, he got in with her. He felt the side of her rump as he slipped deeper inside the bed, experiencing the chill of the fresh linen. He was in bed with an important piece of news. The owner of the most famous unpublished novel in the world.

In the darkness, he let his hand find Cynthia's thighs, and soon he was caressing the area just below her navel and above her pubes. Nothing was said for a while. So he carried on.

"If you're going to do that, do it properly," said Cynthia, tiredly.

Cynthia held Urich's hand and placed it, palm down, over her pubic area.

Urich felt his heart pound. He was back on top of his game.

Then, in a flash, he saw TV cameras, the paparazzi, all of them waiting for him to bang her supremely. And there was no possible way that she – Cynthia – could refuse him this time, after the success that HE had got for her…

He sat up, in the bed, slightly breathless, and drank the rest of his vodka and grapefruit. And then leaned across Cynthia – until a certain part of his anatomy (fully erect) was snagging against her left breast.

"What are you doing?"

"I'm just trying to put my glass down on the bedside table," he said, shuffling noisily.

"Why this side? Why are you leaning across me?"

"Nearly got it," he said.

"Oh bloody hell…you're prodding me in my chin!" she said, irate that Urich was attempting to be fellated in such a cowardly-but-deliberate manner.

"I am sorry," he said, realising that Cynthia's status had risen a little since the evening began. She was too good for him now! He sat up, maudlin – and to exacerbate his feeling of rejection, still slightly vertical. He leaped out of bed and searched for his underpants.

"I've got it!" she said, sobering up remarkably. It seemed as though she had had an epiphany from out of nowhere.

"Got what!?" he said, feeling overly nude – and ridiculous. (It was funny how cocaine and embarrassment were two things that could sober a man in seconds.)

"The next part of the plan…" she whimpered, not sounding sexy anymore.

"What?" Urich said genuinely confused.

And then she said something decidedly odd.

"I know what is to happen to me," Cynthia said, coldly. Her drunkenness was revealing a candour that was self-defeating. This wasn't like her.

Urich became paranoid, which coupled with his nakedness and his recent feeling of rejection made him feel somewhat useless. How did she know what was going to happen to her?

Jonathan knew that Cynthia would have to brace herself for what he was about to say to her; about what he was going to lay on her. It was a bombshell – no doubt about that.

And it wasn't the news about the break-in at the gallery….

He knew she might be mortified by this, but, on the other hand, maybe she would have welcomed this more than he ever could have imagined.

His heart started beating so hard that it gave him a head-rush.

"Cynthia, I know you are not in a million years going to believe this…..

"but …

Urich was on the floor, resting on bare kneecaps, teeth gritted.

"I want to marry you!"

CHAPTER ELEVEN

Urich had not intended to say this.

He was, initially, going to tell her about the theft of the Unread Manuscript ™, but had decided that the news might have sobered her up and killed the romantic milieu that he had so carefully achieved. The marriage proposal was a curveball, a lateral move intended to secure maximum results. (Well, at least a well-deserved roll in the hay.)

But that said: she had, regrettably, fallen asleep; without giving him a definitive answer. He even doubted whether she had remembered him asking.

Were his words that inconsequential?

Urich realised he had been losing valuable time. There was serious work to do. For one, he would have to find out what the fuck had happened to the money supposedly earmarked for Sime Hunst. Also, he knew that he would have to go into work and use a computer there as his one at home had broken down.

He would also need to find his bloody mobile phone.

There was too much uncertainty now; he was drowning in the stuff.

Though he was sure of one fact:-

He was to encounter his little imposter friend again.

But first, he would give his friend at the charity shop a little call.

That was after having a naughty line of Charleston (to sharpen the old senses; just like Sherlock Holmes would've done).

CHAPTER TWELVE

At home, the vicious murderer sat at his computer saddened and perplexed.

He asked himself, clenching his fists, why he was such a shittingly useless pig of a killer and a man. He punched himself in the side of the face.

His computer had sent back all of his emails from the other day; and none had reached their destination. *Useless!!*

Had Urich even got his reprehensible ultimatum? – the killer quite rightly wondered, and became angry, and then decided to have a glass of orange squash.

Maybe he had been too demanding of his new friend. Perhaps, he should have requested that Urich merely cut off one of her ears...make her a member of the Van Gogh Club. And why not? She wanted in, the stupid shit pig girl! She wanted a seat in that exclusive arena, without paying the toll, the fare – which was: pain, self-loathing and, in some cases, extreme violence toward one's self.

He then painted two of the nails on his left hand black. After that he put on a Leonard Cohen CD into his CD player and punched himself in the centre of his own forehead. Then closed his eyes. In bliss.

Before work, Urich paid a visit to the charity shop in Pimlico. His contact, unsurprisingly, was not there. So Urich spoke to a worker there, a fair-haired woman of around 50, and asked about Mark. The woman had confirmed that there was someone called Mark who had done a few days, but she didn't have any contact details for him.

She told Urich she would let Mark know that a nice man had been looking for him.

Urich said not to bother.

"Has the golden boy decided to grace us with one of his rare visits?" said Monty Carn, sardonically, on noticing Urich. They were in the long, narrow corridors of HS&S – standing beneath a painting of the company chairmen.

"Not now fatso!" said Urich.

Carn was instantly angered. His eyes, within seconds, had gone coke-can red. And Urich was amused by this.

Urich tried to second-guess what his adversary was thinking. And concluded: how Carn must have been livid that Urich – against the odds, from out of nowhere – was somehow doing outstandingly-bloody-well.

It must have scorched his soul. Set it on fire.

Consequently, Urich thought to himself if he ever wrote a novel: he would cast a character very similar to Monty Carn, as a fat hairy necrophiliac rapist (and quickly realised that it would be quite hard to rape a dead person).

Urich walked off and left Carn looking crazed; and not smirking for once.

But Carn should have known better: that for today, tomorrow and a little way into the future: it was Urich's time, not his.

Urich asked his part-time assistant to come in.

He sat at his desk, nervously tapping at the desk with his fingernails. As soon as Alexander Trammell had arrived in the room, Urich knew the course of action to take.

"I want you to go through the slushpile and all my e-mails and look for troublemakers, weirdoes, people with a grudge against me. Just put aside anything that strikes you as suspicious."

In two hours, Alexander Tramell – the slender, feckless youth with the side-parting and spots – found eight manuscripts and two e-mail offenders. These all, according to Trammell, merited some investigation.

After a look himself, Urich threw the manuscripts into the bin. "These aren't very good, but they don't need the attention of the police," Urich said, enjoying the insouciance of a joke to soothe his shot nerves. Tramell laughed in sympathy with his superior.

Urich checked the second email ('suspicious' due to its subject title: 'Enjoy this Friend?'), and saw that someone had attached a medium-sized file to it. It was an MPEG. The mail was from actheone@aol.com.

And, curiously, it didn't have a returnable address.

Urich waited a good twenty minutes for the download and watched the pixels evolve into something that made his mouth open gradually – only to close much later.

He had become, for the moment, stuck. As if paralysed.

What was it? he asked himself. But he had suspected what it was. For although it was a poor-resolution playback, it was flesh on the bones of what he feared might be lurking in his closet.

'*Oh my God.*'

He kept on watching himself. At the flat, on that night. With her…and saw how she, that prostitute, was trying to break away from him and then how he had her up against a wall.

'*Oh my fucking god!*'

Urich ran to close the door of his office. So no one could see this footage of him at the South London flat.

He got to thinking fast. Someone was out to destroy him, which made a change from his usual brand of self-sabotage.

What he has seen is essentially a snuff film.

With himself as 'one' of the leading players.

At home, The Thief reads the penultimate chapter of the so-called 'unread' manuscript. This chapter focuses on the activities of someone called X. It's less a piece of writing, he feels, than a comprehensive, analytical piece of surveillance.

X, according to this Unread Manuscript, is to be a victim of a very horrible and deviant crime. X, according to the Manuscript, is going to be savaged and sliced-up by two formidable men. They are also going to 'transgress' with X's dead body.

The Thief skimmed through the text, and saw more...but couldn't process such disgusting revelations.

He threw the manuscript on the floor and felt sickened by what he had read. It was as though someone had punched him in the stomach.

The Thief lit a cigarette (just to get him to take oxygen down in his lungs with the smoke) and wondered when his employer would call again.

He was unhappy about this whole business.

And, moreover, he wondered why the very last chapter of the Unread Manuscript™ had been left blank.

It was Five O'Clock already.

After Tramell had left to go home, Urich decided to look through all the files on his computer. He wanted to double check that Alexander Tramell hadn't missed anything.

He checked the recycle bin, and was surprised at seeing how much stuff was in there. Most of it was just old rubbish, but something drew his attention.

It was an email from *Shitpig*. It was sitting in the bin, unhighlighted, seemingly already read. Someone – not Urich – had been reading his emails. This made Urich both angry and concerned. But more concerned.

Urich clicked on this particular email.

To: jurich@hss.co.uk

From: shitpig (actheone@aol.com)

Subject: Reneging...

Urich, you have a nerve.

I gave you a choice. I told you that you were to kill her or smother her with love. Don't you remember: rape or the grave?

You didn't do either.

You leave me with no choice.

I hope you enjoy your future of pain!

What was he talking about: a choice? Rape and the grave? What was all this?!

Urich became very solemn. He could see that his life was about to take an inexorable path down some place he just didn't want to go.

So why didn't Tramell tell him...warn him about the message. Somebody had read it, hadn't they? But what if he, himself, had opened the message and just not got round to reading it and had put it in the recycle bin and...

He realised that he could no longer trust anybody. And questioned: whether this applied to himself?

His priorities were all wrong, it seemed. He needed to re-evaluate his whole situation, and work out exactly what the hell was going on.

This person now wanted Urich to harm Cynthia. But WHY? Hadn't he taken money from Urich and Zinner? Why was he tormenting Urich like this? Urich had to think fast. What if this madman was not bluffing? And why should he bluff? This man, whoever he was, saw his intentions through to the end – however far-fetched they were. Zinner's purchase of the 'Unread Manuscript' was proof-positive of that. So Urich had to assume this was no idle threat.

So what was he to do? He couldn't kill her nor could he do anything else that was being suggested. Or could he?

He ran into the office bathroom and splashed cold water on his face and saw his reflection in a mirror. It looked like he had been crying, which he never could do. Crying tears was something lost to his youth, a memory. It was academic now.

And then he saw something new in his eyes – something deep, abstruse – something hard to explain.

The first thing he did at his flat was look for the mobile phone that he had mislaid. Once located (it was under his bed), he clamped the rather bulky handset to his head, eyes closed – and imagined the worst.

There was one message from Zinner, one from Alexander Tramell. And another message from a man, possibly foreign, who sounded distressed.

Oh no.

He listened to the message over and over again, and was stunned. Rape and the grave? What was this madman asking him to do?

He considered things, dry-washing his hands nervously. Rape and the grave??

Urich foresaw the metaphorical gun put to his head. He imagined a dark time in the near future. He saw himself assaulting Cynthia to save his own skin, to save himself from the threats of this persistent psychopath.

Then he thought something shameful, absolutely reprehensible. He wondered if he did such a thing: what would happen if she enjoyed it.....and was instantly sickened as he realised that he had arrived at the mindset of a rapist.

Then it occurred to him. How would this madman even know if he had raped Cynthia? He tried to be objective about the situation. Would the madman be watching him? How would he know if he was raping her or just having normal consenting sex? He thought about his past sexual adventures, and conceded that to a passer-by or a voyeur – it would be extremely hard to tell if one of his partners had been consenting or not. He remembered one ex-girlfriend had described his 'style of lovemaking' as "uncoordinated". Another ex had termed his method as "busy". Lucy Kelly, from college, had seen his antics as "bungling and ridiculous".

He laughed at himself and thought about this all some more and started to feel unwell, a touch faint; an ache in the pit of his stomach.

He was looking for answers to questions that kept forming in his head. But an even more pressing question was: how was he going to sleep that night, and exactly when should he involve the police?

If ever?

He had an idea. He would ask Hinds (of Hinds Starkey and Sacks) if he could spend some time at his cottage in Devon. And was this such a ridiculous request? Hinds had previously let Monty Carn use it after selling the film rights to Mike Jones's first novel. Surely Urich deserved the same preferential treatment now?

He was thinking too much and reached for some pills from a container in his pocket, and soon afterwards, chopped out a line of cocaine from an old wrap he'd found in his drawer. He chopped out another line on a current copy of Loaded magazine and thought that if Cynthia and Monty Carn ever got together, he just wouldn't know what to do.

In a fleeting moment, he imagined fighting for Cynthia's honour and hurting Carn really badly. And then he had a distasteful thought (another one).

He imagined being so hurt that he hated Cynthia and, in some horrible mental image: maybe killing her. The coke was accelerating his thinking, and he pondered how 'that' could make headlines for him and his little project, his baby…if she were to perish.

He chopped out another line and made the tranquillisers very redundant.

CHAPTER THIRTEEN

More questions and even less answers.

He re-examined everything that had happened to him since meeting Sime Hunst's imposter on that sordid night. And became confounded and depressed. Should he try and look for the flat that he had gone to that night? Or a more pertinent question: where in hell was it? He wouldn't even know where to start looking.

He popped another two diazepam pills and made a promise to himself: to not become hysterical, and just be calm.

He needed to be methodical about all this. Though his head seemed too cluttered with 'just everything'. He was thinking too fast.

Cynthia felt bad about turning Urich down, and put his marriage offer down to the alcohol, and all the recent excitement. She was flattered, perhaps – but was more tired than anything. She needed beauty sleep for the interview with She Magazine. Not that she wanted to attend. In fact, she would tell Zinner's PA that, from now on, she was going to be a recluse.

Cynthia went to bed and turned off her bedside light and wondered where all this publicity would take her. She imagined all kinds of nice places that she could go in the world – like very hot places – but skiing was something she truly wanted to do. She thought of a pony her dad once owned, and being brunette again, and likes the way some girls from Islington have their hair. A change would be good but…then she thinks of nice things like ice cream, hunky boys and chocolate…

She was asleep.

It was later. How much later, she was not sure and her eyes were slow and unfocused. Then a sudden noise woke her up, startled her into consciousness. It sounded like some heavy boxes falling down near to the front door. She thought quickly, her heart thumping right in her ears, deafening her. She stood up in her bedroom. In the dark.

She opened the bedroom door slowly and slunk out onto the landing, in bare feet, stumbling against the banister. She switched on the hall lights.

"Who goes there?" she said with mock bravado, and trembled. She spoke again, and her words felt like someone else's. No one answered.

On the doormat was a package.

It had been left by someone. Put through her letterbox.

CHAPTER FOURTEEN

The killer Andrei was combing his shoulder-length grey hair, and sat before a mirror in the bedroom. He observed himself and squinted his eyes, reminding himself slightly of Bryan Ferry, but with a longer face and a more prominent chin.

He knows he is not a wildly attractive man and is pleased that he is not a narcissist like that shittingly insipid boy Urich. Nor is he Helen of Troy – whose beautiful face launched a thousand ships. His appeal is to elicit fear. Carpov's ugly mug will launch a thousand shits!

Andrei is fed up with his contemporaries and their unsubtlety – their scant sense of dignity. Who is he talking about? Serial killers who think they can write. Firstly, they get caught and then have the lack of dignity to not keep quiet about their activities. So who are Andrei's contemporaries – these braggards? One is the fucking whore Mary Bell who has been paid by an international publisher to boast about her wicked life to some old woman. Another is that grinning asshole OJ. And there are others.

Andrei doesn't know these people, these killers, as such, but he knows they are getting more notoriety than him – and he suspects, somehow, that they are all getting paid more money than him. He knows that the tabloids and publishers have no qualms about shoving their chequebooks in their greedy tormented faces. Deary me – he considers – they're even giving blank cheques to thuggish East End hard men like Mad Frankie Fraser and his ilk (although Andrei feels better about himself compared to these terrors). You see, Andrei even is shocked by their disgusting, bloodthirsty antics. Sometimes he cries, but then he cries about how beautiful some acts of violence are. But enough of that.

Andrei sits at the kitchen table running a sharp, serrated knife over his knuckles and thinks how much of a cliché it is, doing such a thing, but does it anyway. Then he thinks about how no one – like the media – really talks about him. Because HE is still at large, still not caught. They talk about all the jokers who were caught: Hindley, Nielson, Brady and all those insane Americans. They don't deserve any notoriety, because…because the useless fools got darn well caught!! They are amateurs – clearly! But I am not!!

Carpov begins to cry endlessly…

When Andrei composes himself, he reminds himself that he is crying for nothing. Because he has got what he wants. And how is that? Because that foolhardy young man Urich has given him a whole load of readies. Then he thinks how clever he is for cashing in while he is still going strong, still doing it. So clever clever, and he dances: spinning, a real whirling dervish of evil and energy. Then he decides that he will keep to his word and find that scrawny young woman and make her wish that she had never been born.

You see that pretty young woman had broken the terms of the agreement, he thinks. The whole world was witness to that. N'est ce pas?

And Urich has not dealt with the matter, which leaves him with no choice but to deal with the situation himself.

But first he stands in front of the mirror, wide-legged, and tries to look as diabolical as possible. He says a few choice words ("I will slay you, shitpig!") in a voice that could be described as canine, husky and truly diabolical.

It is time to reveal himself, fully, to their world.

PART 3

CHAPTER FIFTEEN

Cynthia picked up the brown package and opened it. The trembling began again, as she wondered who could have sent her a blank VHS videotape. And why? And at night!

But what if the package had been there already – she thought, trying to comfort herself.

She knew one thing for certain: all the doors and windows were going to be tightly shut, and the curtains drawn...and the TV turned up loud. But, at the back of her mind, something else was niggling. The house seemed colder than it had before, and she was convinced there was a breeze.

Had she left a window open?

She would need to check every room in her house. She went upstairs to the bathroom and saw something that almost stopped her heart from pumping any more blood.

It was the window; it had been opened by someone other than herself.

Fear was flooding her brain now; making her eyesight blur. The unwelcome breeze had raised an alarm that someone might be on the landing...and then she heard a noise coming from outside. Like a can had got knocked over. She looked out of the open window and saw how a wooden ladder – not hers – was leaning against the garden side of her house. She leaned out further and watched the garden. She saw the trees and the flowers and the fence at the rear of the garden. And in a small corner of the garden, bathed in a little light from a nearby street lamp, she was positive that she saw a figure hiding in the corner of the garden. She phoned Urich, and hoped to God he would answer.

Within seven or eight minutes, he was there to support her.

"Jonathan, you're here...so soon?" she said, surprised.

"I was in the area, thank God," Urich said, a little flustered, and touched her arm sensitively.

She looked at him, kind of puzzled.

He told her to stay in the kitchen, and make a cup of tea: to not be scared. Then he found a large bulky torch and ventured out into the garden, wearing that look he had cultivated for so long, that combination of modesty, valour and total pluck. Cynthia now watched from the kitchen window.

With a straightened back and his chin raised higher than usual, he walked halfway down the lawn and, pointing his torch – boldly, and yet intrepidly – he illuminated the far corner of the garden. And then thought he could see something: someone crouch! Then move!... But when he moved closer, he saw that it was a trick of the light.

There was nothing, just earth. Maybe a few weeds. But ostensibly nothing. No bogeyman. No hiding, crouching, twisted figure.

But something, a few metres away, caught Urich's attention.

It was a crumpled note with someone's handwriting. He picked up the note and straightened it out against the flatness of his palm. And read it. It said: *Why did you kill me? I had nothing and you killed me? Was I not important enough in your world?*

Then Urich saw a metal box by some carnations. It was shoebox shaped. He put his hand on the box and was about to...

He heard a scream, coming from the house. It was Cynthia, screaming in a way that Urich had never heard before – except in films. Her fear had paralysed him, made his legs cumbersome, awkward.

Cynthia continued to scream. So Urich made his way into the house, leaving the metal box in the garden.

The TV was on and something was playing. A video.

Once in the living room, Urich knew he must stop her from seeing what was on the tape and ejected it from the VCR. But where was Cynthia!? He went to look for her, and found her cradling herself on the floor of the kitchen: embryonic, trying to make herself unseen.

"Did you see who it was?"

Cynthia, as white as a sheet, just shook her head.

There was no question about it. Someone had been in the house. And behind Cynthia's whimpering, Urich could hear the faint shambles of someone scarpering down the street.

In the morning, he insisted that Cynthia must get the hell out of London; and was worried that she might have seen something on the tape, but was fairly sure she hadn't. He told her to pack some things, and be quick about it.

(But why would Cynthia, so readily, agree to come with him if she'd seen what was on the cassette? This convinced him that she was in the dark about the footage.)

They drove down to Urich's flat with the intention of picking up some clothes and towels, etc. But once inside the flat, Urich became suspicious that someone might have somehow got in, so he had a look around the flat.

There was no evidence of any breaking and entering.

He checked his letters: a BT bill, another bill, junk mail... and one brown envelope unstamped, undated.

Hurriedly, he opened it. Inside were two A4 mono laser prints. He looked and looked and wasn't quite sure what he was seeing. The images were faint, faded. He narrowed his eyes. There are bodies, he thinks, laid out on tables; like someone has taken pictures in a mortuary. Some of the bodies are not all there, parts missing. It looks like one of the bodies has been covered in paint.

In another photograph: there's a bird's-eye-view photo of a metal box, with the lid next to it. Inside the same box, there is a severed (female) human ear. Urich's neck tightened, or seemed to. His breathing felt constricted.

Then: he heard the dring, dring of his mobile phone, and picked it up. The line went dead. Someone was messing with him, taunting him. He stuffed the prints into the envelope and carried the envelope under his arm. He would keep the metal box in the boot of his car.

"Is my life in danger?" Cynthia asked.

"No, but we must err on the side of caution."

"What the hell is going on, Jonathan?!"

Urich didn't answer her.

"Is this anything to do with me signing the..the...thing in my blood?"

Urich didn't answer her.

"Have you informed the police?!"

Urich said he had.

Urich said that everything would be alright if they just got out of London.

Just until it all blew over.

"It?" Said Cynthia.

Urich didn't answer her.

They got into Urich's white clapped-out BMW, and Urich explained how he had arranged some time off. And how? Because he was still the golden boy of Hinds Starkey and Sacks and 'could get way with murder', as far as any of them were concerned.

Anyhow, Cynthia appeared to feel safer in his company. It was preferable, at least, to being alone in her flat.

It had stopped raining. They had been driving for over an hour: all winding roads, the smell of clean country air and damp winds. They were listening to an audio book cassette of Jack Kerouac's On The Road, read by some American who seemed familiar, but obscure: Carradine, David? It was boring as hell. Though the American's downbeat temperate voice made Urich feel calmer and

Cynthia, too, appeared to enjoy its sleep-inducing effect. The drive was also good for Urich's sense of panic. He popped another pill.

After a while, Urich was breathing deep unhurried breaths. Privately, in his mind, he was saluting the tranquillisers; drafting out a thank-you letter to the MD of the firm who made them. The smoky voice from the audio cassette seemed to make him less anxious. He was happy for a minute, until he remembered the footage of him-and-the-girl, and tried to concentrate on the driving. His vision was beginning to haze a little. It was definitely the medication.

"You have told the Police, haven't you?" Cynthia said, with just one eye open. Her face was creased from sleeping against the car seat.

"Yes," said Urich, and while coaxing the steering wheel to the left, glanced over at Cynthia again. He felt kind of protective. He studied her a while and took his eye off the road.

She looked marvellous, he decided. And it was great – he thought – that she was back to wearing a skirt again. But what was... this?

Urich detected the faintest hint of stubble on her bare legs.

Jesus, he thought. He saw tiny flecks on her shins, and knew that she had let things slide. And felt pissed off.

Something had happened to her. A spell, or something, had been cast over her. Something was not quite right. And the way she had been talking earlier: saying she'd like to be more political. She said she didn't like the Tory party anymore. She kept talking about how she wanted to write a column for The Guardian; write about her experience of being 'Lizzy'.

She went on for another four minutes, talking all about herself.

"I'm even thinking of writing a novel," she said.

"Why are you talking like this?" exclaimed Urich, utterly confused.

"Like what?"

"I don't know you seem different?"

Cynthia pulled a face, as if he had farted.

Urich had clearly said something stupid, but wondered why she was being so uppity all of a sudden.

"I want to write for real, not just pretend," she said earnestly.

Urich was noticeably irritated and held the steering wheel with both hands, for once, and focused back on the road. It was proving difficult, though, keeping his mind on the driving. He was too busy trying to come to terms with the new cocky her – wanting to *write* for real. What had fucking got into her? He thought about this some more and concluded that she had reached some kind of personality crisis. I mean who did she think she was?

More importantly, who did he think he was? Everything was combining and conspiring to pervert his normally genial personality. He started thinking about guilt, evil and the need to confess – and then about losing his fucking mind...

"Watch what you're doing...you're beginning to veer into the side of the road!"

Urich knew the pills were to blame, but he couldn't help being distracted by the idiocy of her own actions...

And then she really did it. She really fucking did it.

She started talking about Monty Carn, when she should have known not to; and spoke of how sensitive Monty Carn could be.

Urich bit his lower lip.

She said that she liked to read books that were sad and see movies that made her cry, and said how she could really talk about sensitive subjects with Monty. Like he wasn't afraid to show another, more feminine side to himself...

"I CAN MAKE YOU CRY?!" shouted Urich, louder than intended. He was really zoning out.

"I mean Monty took me to the cinema and we watched a French film together and both of us sat there and wept. And it was so weird because I only cried out of my left eye, as he was sitting on my right hand side...it was as if I was shy of crying in front of him...it's silly, I know."

Urich sighed and thought there was something shame-faced about doing such a thing, hidden by darkness. He imagined Carn with tears coming out of his twisted smiling chops, *like some weird weeping mouth*?

He then thought about how immature they both were, crying.

And became increasingly angry that he couldn't do something like that.

He felt ridiculously shallow.

And then he pined for her old self, her previous idiotic self. The self that *Might* let him get what he wanted.

(He wondered if it was, indeed, right not to contact the police just yet.)

CHAPTER SIXTEEN

The Thief was not sure what to do. He had a bag of someone's body-parts in the boot of his car and probably the most famous unpublished novel in the history of the entire planet in a cupboard in his basement.

But still no mention of the burglary at the gallery. And still no call from his boss about what to do next. He just had to wait, he supposed.

He paced the kitchen and descended the stairs that lead to the basement, and opened the cupboard that housed the manuscript. There it was. There was the blue-bound manuscript, in his hands. So he stood there – with the lights on, but with a torch nearby, just in case the lights were to suddenly go out – and started to read the thing some more.

He turned to the first page, catching his shadow on the wall, and thought that the amount of light in his basement was pretty low. He could hardly read anything: as if the text had faded; as if it was a poor photocopy. He turned to another page, and the same again. The type had faded, pretty much, so the page was white but faintly mottled with the memory of something. Another page, it was the same. And another, the same yet again. The Thief didn't know what was happening.

110

But later, after calling an expert on the matter, he did.

The person who printed out this manuscript had, presumably, used a fading ink.

Shit – he thinks. Now nobody will believe him about the body that he found in the woods. And it would be just his luck if he got framed for the murders explained in the manuscript.

Real murders that exist, not just in someone's head.

The phone began to ring....

Was it his employer, he speculated, with the new instructions?

They arrived at Hind's cottage when it was still dark. It was an old-fashioned place, made of dark-red bricks and set on a small hill.

Cynthia thought it "quaint", and Urich, having just parked up, hoped it would be medicine for his rattled mind. He needed to not think. About anything.

A dash of rain made them both excited and huddle in front of the door, as Urich searched for the key. A bleep and a buzz inside Urich's coat pocket announced a new text message. He stood next to a much less-stressed Cynthia, and stole a quick a look at the missive.

He shut his eyes in disgust. It was Hunst's imposter, but he would pretend, to himself, that it was not. Urich would not allow this situation to capsize him. No, he would turn his attentions to pleasant things: like being here with Cynthia.

This was not the time to fall apart and become victim. The object of the exercise was to relax, recharge the old batteries. Take advantage of old man Hind's hospitality.

Still, at the same time, Urich was aware that he would need to be on his guard. At all times.

It was an hour or so later, after they had settled in.

It was morning now, and the sun was out.

Cynthia walked past in her T-Shirt and knickers, lit up by a beam of light from the living room window, and Urich couldn't help noticing.

"I'm going to have a shower," she said striding past him with her bare legs. And then she returned to Urich, who was slumped in a leather armchair. She stood over him, looking down: "Why have you still got your coat on?"

Urich had, in actual fact, put his overcoat back on just a few minutes before. It made him feel safer. It was kind of odd how anxiety inspired him to put on more layers. He supposed that it beefed him up, made him feel more of a force to be reckoned with, however weak he was feeling inside. Cynthia, in contrast, seemed to put less on – regardless of her emotional state. That was just her.

She eventually left the room and Urich began pacing around again. He went into the kitchen and had a drink of water. His mouth was dry and he began to feel sick.

He needed to throw up and, removing his overcoat, rushed to find a lavatory.

After ten minutes, Cynthia shouted out to him from the stairs.

"Jonathan, it's your mobile phone!"

Urich had left it in the kitchen. Desperately, with his face still dripping with water, he burst into Hind's kitchen and saw the phone, by the sink. It was ringing. He stood there, fixed to the spot.

"Jesus! Pick it up, why don't you?"

Cynthia, in a towel, elbowed Urich out of the way, and picked up the phone for him. Barefoot, she walked into the corner of the small kitchen and pressed the phone to her ear.

Urich prayed hard and clenched his fists, hoping that...

"It's for you. One of your friends...."

Cynthia handed him the phone and left to have her shower.

Urich frowned and knew the person on the other end of the phone wasn't a friend; Urich had none.

"Are you ready for what comes next?" said the voice. It was faint. "I'm going to make the game a little easier for you. Forget my previous wishes. You have a new choice now...I suggest you carry out one of the options. Or DIE!"

Urich listened intently.

"You can molest the bitch. OR you can cut her ear off. And Urich...you can say you were trying to shave her legs and...and the razor...just SLIPPED!"

Urich pressed the off button with his thumb, and saw how his hands were trembling. *Had Carpov been watching them? Was he nearby? Or had Urich just imagined all this?*

Ignore it all, he thought. Just ignore.

Urich had a wash and returned downstairs, clean shaven and dressed in a French Connection shirt and faded jeans. The stress that he had felt earlier had subsided and he felt more composed; with less of a need to wear his heavy overcoat.

Cynthia had also changed into a something more conservative: a much longer denim skirt and a cashmere sweater. Urich acknowledged that Cynthia seemed so delicate and fragile, despite her self-assurance and opinions. And he felt, thinking about it, more protective over her. But at the same time, Urich felt clumsy and aware of his physicality – which lead him to try and keep out of her way.

He needed to compose himself, become rational again.

Later on, Urich – who had eaten a small piece of hash, as chaser to a cocktail of different-coloured tablets – made the tea, and explained to Cynthia how much he liked Devon and "its rustic charm". Cynthia said how much she did too, and Urich continued to say how he enjoyed "the fresh air, and the salty breeze drifting up from the sea", and both parties seemed momentarily at peace with their curious situation.

No one mentioned the obvious. Everyone kept off the subject of Cynthia's previous intruder. But Urich, who was beginning to feel strangely relaxed, had predicted a storm of sorts; and wasn't clear about what was going to happen next. But he was very sure that something very nasty was waiting for them.

Or maybe just her.

He looked out the kitchen window and marvelled at how blue the sky was. From the manuscripts that got sent into him over the last year, he had accumulated many ways of describing a blue sky. A blue sky could be azure or cobalt or even sapphire. But he liked to think of it as just blue.

They both smoked cigarettes and Urich – mourning the loss of past ignorance – wished for the days when he was less culturally significant. But that wasn't all that was on his mind. He kept recollecting things: fragments, aural snippets especially from that night of meeting the fake Hunst. It all was getting to him, this constant running through of things....

He had another cigarette directly after his last had gone out.

With their cups of tea in front of them, they faced the blazing log fire, sitting in a leather armchair each. Urich looked over at Cynthia, and Cynthia, quite often, was too tired to notice his constant glances. He wanted to tell her about how stoned and confused he was feeling, but didn't want her to see him as weak.

She seemed a little self-conscious, Urich thought – and felt that she was feeling a bit insecure being with him. It was silly really as they had known each other for a quite a long time.

After searching in her handbag, Cynthia started to apply some make-up, and asked about the manuscript.

"I wouldn't know what was in it," he said, "because I haven't read it all..yet."

Cynthia then wanted to know whether many people would come to the gallery to see it. She wanted to know how it was going to be presented: the Unread Manuscript.

"What's there to see?" said Urich. "I don't think anybody in their right mind would be that interested in it."

"Don't you believe in it?" said Cynthia – a pitying glaze resplendent in her bottle-green eyes. "You're so cynical, aren't you?" she added, quite irked, and Urich did not answer.

A silence loomed large, and Urich could hear birdsong in the distance. It sounded kind of disturbing.

"Do you even like reading books?" Cynthia asked.

"What?"

Urich thought about it. No, he didn't if he was to be honest with himself. *Reading was obsolete due to the continued significance of the soaps and reality TV* – Urich had read somewhere, once.

Sure, he had read a bit of Hemingway and Faulkner back then for A level, but he would much rather watch a DVD film from Blockbuster or play a shoot-em-up on his computer.

He could tell she was pissed off with him, and, again, he cursed his problem of speaking without judging what effect it might have on someone.

They sat some more in front of the antique fireplace.

After watching the blues and reds dance around the yellow flames, Urich then asked her if she had regretted becoming involved with the venture.

Cynthia paused, and pondered the question.

Surprisingly, her normally straight mouth curved; and grew into a private smile.

CHAPTER SEVENTEEN

The Thief knew that the only person who could explain anything to him: was Urich.

Seeing as his boss was incommunicado – his main hope was to find Urich, as he had reason to suspect that Urich had answers for many of his questions. And why did he think that?

The manuscript had told him so, and, apparently, the manuscript did not lie. The rotting body in the boot of his car was proof of that.

It was 3am. Urich had been sleeping lightly and was finally awoken by a noise from outside the cottage. He had been dreaming about rain. He turned to look at Cynthia's bed (which was in the same room as his own), and saw that the covers and sheets had been pulled back, and she was not to be seen.

In silence, Urich walked down the stairs of the cottage and entered the living room. There he saw Cynthia, dressed in a white dressing gown sitting in front of the blazing log fire. Closer-up, it appeared that she was asleep in the armchair, and in her hand was a tea cup. Urich approached her, tip-toeing, and saw that the cup was half-full with tea. Turning towards the other armchair nearest the lamp, he saw something funny. Or funny to him.

On the table next to the armchair, next to the lamp…was another cup.

The porcelain cup, like Cynthia's, was half-full.

He touched the mug and it was still very warm. Carefully, without making a sound, he touched the cup in Cynthia's hand, moving as softly as possible (without waking her). It was warm too. Why would she would make herself two cups of tea at roughly the same time?

Had someone been there at the cottage with Cynthia: drinking tea with her?

Urich looked at his watch and noted that it was 3.30 in the morning.

My God! It had just come to him, as he looked at the cup in a different light. Without doubt, this was the clincher: he'd suddenly noticed that only one of the cups had a faint lipstick mark on it. Surely, if both cups were hers – then both of them would have been marked with the same lipstick smudge?

(Or was this another sign that he was losing his grip on reality?)

Maybe, later, over breakfast, she would explain all. Regale him with the most pedestrian of tales. Maybe he had just been on edge; been too distrusting.

Everything had gotten out of control. In a split-second, he wished to turn back the clock to a time where there was something comforting about not doing so well. Being unremarkable. Being unwatched.

He carefully took the cup out of her hand, and placed it on a table and went back up the stairs.

Urich hardly slept at all after that; and waited for her to awake. He wanted to know what was really going on.

Urich wanted to ask her if anyone had been in the cottage with her. But he wouldn't just yet.

He would test her first. That is what he would do.

Cynthia was fussing with the cutlery and seemed hypnotised by the clock on the wall. She had most definitely changed – (Urich was watching her closely and analysing her everry move).

He saw that a smile was on Cynthia's face, and watched as she brushed her short blonde hair back in a conceited manner. Then he became aware of a tense expression on her face.

Now was the time to employ the ace up his dressing gown sleeve. Urich, rather cleverly, asked her to make him a cup of tea. She said yes, reluctantly – until she noticed that he had a cup on the table that was still three-quarters full with tea. Urich, still watching her, raised the cup to his mouth and took a sip (careful not to burn his lips).

Cynthia said nothing, and the tense expression on her face became exaggerated. This prompted him to say what was on his mind.

"Last night you made yourself two cups of tea…at the same time? WHY!?"

"No, not quite," said Cynthia.

"I only like a hot drink when it's hot. If a drink cools down too much…well, I don't like it. I make myself another one… …straight away."

Urich was stumped momentarily. Was her answer acceptable? *She was lying: both cups of tea were very warm, weren't they!?*

"I want to go home now," said Cynthia, seated at the kitchen table –uninterested in Urich's reasoning.

"You can't", said Urich.

"Why?"

"Because, it's still not safe."

Cynthia seemed flummoxed by Urich's behaviour, and was becoming tired by his game playing. Urich, most probably, was acting like a paranoid prick, and he could understand her wanting to get away from him for a while. Apparently, she wanted fresh air and he could see no reason to prevent her from getting some.

He opened the front door of the cottage for her, and watched her walk outside. He saw her smoke a cigarette next to his parked car. She was still in her dressing gown and visibly stressed.

She appeared, though, to be plotting something.

CHAPTER EIGHTEEN

There was a knock at the door of the cottage. An insistent knock.

Urich, now dressed, opened the door, assuming it would be Cynthia and was surprised when the door did open, revealing someone different.

Someone he had seen before.

Many times before.

The person stood there in front of him.

Urich didn't know what to say, and was lost for words.

The person was sobbing and, unexpectedly, tears were cascading, meandering down those reddened cheeks. The man walked forward, causing Urich to take steps backwards.

"Why are you crying?" Urich said, when he was really thinking: why are you even standing here like this? Why are YOU here?

Urich – his mind whirring, the cogs revolving very fast – wondered what his purpose was, him being here.

It was Hinds. The big boss. He of Hinds Starkey and Sacks.

He with the scary, serious face.

He with the unkempt fair hair. He who looked like a younger, slimmer version of Winston Churchill. He with breath that

121

smelt of stale cigar smoke, and those deep-set eyes sunk inside the plump white face.

"Sir? What are you doing here?"

Hinds – the grand, austere man that Urich had come to fear so often – was crying unashamedly.

"I must talk to you, my youngsters..?"

At this moment, Cynthia entered the house and stood behind Urich. She watched as Hinds and Urich shook hands firmly, in a display of faint emotion.

"Things have gotten out of control," said Hinds, sitting down at the kitchen table and smoking the end of a thin cigar. "Andrew Carp has come back home to make all our lives a misery."

"Andrew Carp?"

"Well, you might know him as Andrei Carpov."

"I don't know any Andrei Carpov?" said Urich, rashly.

"Well I think you should, dearest boy," said Hinds with understanding, sad eyes.

Urich paced around the kitchen, walking backwards and forwards. He was shallow-breathing and trying to overcome an adrenalin rush. He tried to light a cigarette but the lighter's flint wouldn't catch.

"You see Carp is very clever. Much cleverer than you or I!" Hinds put his cigar out in a silver ashtray, and started to cough.

"Well, who is this man?"

Hinds, blotted his forehead with an off-white silk handkerchief, and told of a man who used to work with him at the

122

literary agency, back in the early days. He became clearly distressed, as he related the tale – perspiring, and coughing nervously.

Carp was once a dashing, energetic young blade. A real wit, explained Hinds. That was until he started thinking he was smarter than some of the greatest minds of his generation. Carp had turned down work sent to him by Jean Genet and Samuel Beckett. He'd even scoffed at an early play by Harold Pinter. Eventually, due to his "gross arrogance", writers had left in their droves. The agency – then in its infancy – had lost alot of much-needed business.

"Single-handedly he nearly finished us all off," gasped Hinds, his throat parched of moisture.

He had become a pariah within the industry – Hinds informed.

All of a sudden, his erudition, his wit counted for nothing. He was regarded as a philistine – a big, flatulent joke. Within a short time, Hinds had asked him to leave the agency.

That was when the trouble started.

His instruction to leave the agency had been met by, initially, denial and then plain obstinacy. Carp was a big man and began to use his brawn to intimidate employees and writers alike. He became obsessed, fixed on destroying the reputation of Hinds Starkey and Sacks. Towards the end of the sixties, his twisted and ugly behaviour had become the stuff of legend. But these renowned adventures had already become a serious embarrassment to Hinds Starkey and Sacks.

"I mean…who could tolerate having a six-foot longhaired brute throwing rubbish from bins into the foyer of the agency."

Hinds told of how writers were spat at; women flashed at.

123

"The man was out of control!"

Hinds hands were shaking and something clearly flashed across his mind, as he sat motionless, with fast-moving nervous eyes.

"Oh my god…and there was a time when I employed two people to make him desist from what he was doing. The men I had paid to sort out Carp were a father and his eldest son – a pair of furious bastards: tattooed, real hard men. On one occasion they laughed at him in the street outside the agency. They were calling all the names under the sun and were about to beat him to within an inch of his mad old life…".

"Then what happened?" Cynthia asked, her green eyes big with impatience.

"He faced off these thugs. And he started smiling a grin so big and so wicked and undid his trousers and showed them what he had down there. And with utter nonchalance, he took out a comb from the pocket of his peasouper coat and began combing his lank greasy hair, smiling all the time."

"What did the men do?" Urich asked.

"The thugs had never seen anything like it…and they began to walk the other way…from this six foot lunatic with his ungodly thing out, casually combing his hair back like some obscene teddy boy! Carp followed them and, without saying a word, stabbed the father with an extremely sharp knife produced from his back pocket. He fucked him proper with the knife…as if he were getting aroused from it and kept fucking him until his knife was dripping blood all over the pavement. The most alarming thing was that he…."

"He what?"

"Carp, er, had an erection," said the old man, shamefully. "One onlooker had actually vomited."

What Urich found particularly alarming about the tale was the fact that Hinds, a man who never resorted to bad language, had used the word 'fuck' twice. That was the first time that he had ever heard Hinds swear. And to crown it all: he was describing another man's erection; and sexual violence that was outlandish and nauseating.

Urich could hardly bear to look at Hinds any longer.

Hinds continued. "He has been harassing me for years. It's an on and off thing. More off than on, fortunately, I suppose," he said vaguely.

"But how do you know that Carpov or whateverhescalled is after us?"

"Because Andrew Carp has been sending instructions. He has been in touch with his diseased and bloody instructions. And he will not rest until those orders are carried out!"

"I know what we have to do?! said Cynthia. "We have to call the police!"

But Urich couldn't afford any of that attention.

While Cynthia and Urich argued about the best course of action to take, Hinds stood up and said he had to leave, as he needed to be in Germany for the next day.

Before he left, he gave Urich some advice.

"Jonathan, my boy…if he does get to you and things do get out of control…there is something you can do…to disable him in a way."

"What is that?"

"Just say the words 'Terence Rattigan'. Don't ask why my boy, but these words can halt him, stop him in his tracks."

"Why though?"

"If the situation arises, promise me that you will say these words?"

Urich promised, and shook Hinds by his chubby-but-eminent hand.

He advised Urich to go somewhere where he would be protected. This cottage wouldn't do – as if Carpov did find them, Hinds reckoned, they would not only be helpless, "but most probably well and truly fucked!"

"If I was you, I'd get some police protection," Hinds muttered, dabbing his moist forehead with a handkerchief. "I'd get back into London."

But Urich knew he couldn't involve the police.

It was daybreak. Cynthia was asleep in the passenger seat and Urich, eating an apple, was steering the BMW hastily down the motorway, away from all those past delusions and suspicions. It was time to stay rational.

After driving for around two hours, as fast as he thought he could get away with – he hoped to formulate some kind of cohesive, half-decent plan inside his head. But he'd thought of nothing inspirational. Instead, he smoked a cigarette, and tried to blow smoke rings.

He was thinking about the night he first met Hunst's impostor. It was at that bar: the Bitter Lemon. He was trying to establish exactly how Carpov, if it was indeed him, had hoodwinked him into thinking he was the artist Sime Hunst. These things happened, for sure. It wasn't that he had been exceptionally gullible, was it?

But then he remembered. He remembered that it was, in fact, 'Cynthia' who had definitely told him that it was Sime Hunst in the first place. It had come back to him. Or had he remembered it wrong?

He lit another cigarette and concentrated some more.

"What's that?" said Cynthia, one eye half-opened. It was a rattling sound. Urich turned down the radio, sucked in some smoke from his fag, and listened. It sounded as though they had a flat tyre. "There it goes again."

Once onto a less-busy road, Urich pulled the car over. He took a torch from out of the glove compartment and shone the light on each tyre. The tyre nearest Cynthia was buggered. Completely flat.

Urich went over to the boot and yanked it up high in the air, and stepped back slowly, putting his fingers to his mouth.

There was something there. In the boot. Something unexpected. Something that hadn't been there before.

"Cynthia! Come out here!"

Cynthia, shivering from the cold, peered closer at the square brown cardboard box; about the size of a football.

"Aren't you going to open it?"

Urich trembled, just a little, and took a 6-inch kitchen knife out of his jacket pocket and surprised Cynthia with it. Muttering

127

something to himself, he got to work with the blade, unpicking the masking tape from off the package. After a couple of minutes, he had stripped the package of almost all the tape.

Savagely, he pulled open the flaps of the packaging and Cynthia stood behind him, peering over his shoulder.

"Oh my God, oh my dear God!"

It was the smell that hit them first.

Inside the packaging was a decapitated head; with a liver complexion, congealed shitty-red blood, and eyes shut. The head – with its frightful, rictus grin – appeared to be laughing at them.

Urich saw cheese-yellow flesh, thick veins, and was almost sick.

And they both knew its previous owner.

"Monty!" Cynthia started screaming, with clenched fists, and drool was hanging from her open mouth.

They both clutched hold of each other, and Urich started to tremble. He could hardly talk. The shock must have paralysed his vocal chords. Cynthia gripped hold of his lapels with a strength that had previously been unimaginable. She held him close to her.

The devastating shock of what lay in that package was a warning. A warning to both of them.

Urich kept thinking about the messages from the madman, the signing of the contract. He thought about the video, about the night in the flat…with the girl, the snuff footage. He thought about EVERYTHING and was unable to breath air into his lungs. He felt that he was about to faint.

But then the strangest thing happened. Through his fear, through the sheer horror of it all – he became slightly aroused by being in such close proximity to Cynthia. He didn't have a hard-on, as such. But he was clearly experiencing a pleasing sensation – a warmth, possibly – as he felt the swell of her bosom against his chest. He felt virile, protective over her. Or perhaps, he was simply trying to think of nice pleasurable things to exorcise the repulsion of what he had seen in the car boot. Regardless, he could feel her racing heartbeat, and her breath was slightly sour on his face (but not unpleasant). He wanted to stick his tongue inside her mouth.

At that moment, a car approached. It had come from the same direction that they had driven from. The red car stopped about thirty yards up the road, revving and purring its engine. It was a hatchback, nothing flash or out of the ordinary.

Both Cynthia and Urich stared at the car and waved their arms.

The car started up and inched backward, slowly and cautiously.

Urich ran up to the car and signalled for the car not to drive off. They needed help and it was imperative not to scare anyone.

Urich went to the driver's side of the car and a window was wound down, and then Urich signalled for Cynthia to come along. As Cynthia jogged along, Urich met her halfway and told her to not say a thing. She was to keep her mouth shut about what had just happened.

In the car, the driver who was in his forties and sporting a long beard, asked if everything was "OK?"; and Urich, panicking, didn't want to scare his new lift away with the truth. So – improvising, quite unnecessarily – he made up a story about how someone had been bumping them off the road, playing "silly buggers" with them. Urich said to the driver that they just needed to get into London. Or get to a train station.

Cynthia was shaking and the driver had turned around to see if she was alright.

On the backseat was a tartan rug, and she managed to disguise her trembling beneath it. The driver still seemed uncomfortable, and a little apprehensive.

Urich began to make small talk.

"What do you do?" he asked the driver.

"I'm an artist," replied the driver.

"An artist?" Just what Urich needed right now.

"Would I know you?"

"You might?" replied the driver.

"What's your name? asked Urich.

"It's…I'm not telling you…," said the driver to an overwhelming silence which seemed to make Urich feel light-headed.

The driver began to laugh as he steered his Nissan a little to the left of the lane. And his laugh ended. Stopped, abruptly.

The ensuing silence became more menacing, more attention-grabbing.

It was then that the driver removed his beard and turned around to face a petrified Urich.

"Oh no, no, no" uttered Urich nervously. He could not prevent himself from revealing his private horror to the stranger.

Ignoring Urich's pathetic mantra, the driver kept on driving, and increased his speed – without taking his eyes off the open road. He was smiling and appeared to be enjoying the effect he was having on his passengers.

"Are you Carp?" whispered Urich, leaning way from the driver; his heart hammering inside his chest. At that moment, he couldn't quite recall what Carp, in his previous disguise, had looked like.

"What?"

"Who are you?"

"Well, actually I am called The Detective. I have been sent to help you."

"By whom"

"My Employer."

Urich was worrying, acutely, about the real prospect of having a heart attack. This was starting to get to him. "Please…what is really going on?" he demanded of the man who was in the driving seat, next to him. "Are you going to kill us?"

"No, nothing that severe," said the man in an eloquent voice. *But what did he have in mind that was marginally less severe!?*

Urich knew that he needed to keep his wits about him, despite the fact that the driver did not look particularly intimidating. Quite the opposite: this bespectacled man, who had been initially polite, was slight in build and quite a few years older than Urich. He had brown hair that was slightly-receding. And there was something quite unremarkable about him. Urich could imagine him being a biologist or someone who worked for Westminster Council.

"Why are you called The Detective?" asked Urich.

"It's just a codename."

The Thief (for it was really him) continued to drive and, clicked his fingers all of a sudden. It seemed as though he had just remembered something. He took an audio cassette from the pocket of his white shirt and slotted it into the car's cassette recorder.

In a few seconds, Cynthia and Urich were treated to a compilation of songs from a heavy, weird progressive-rock band that Urich didn't know or understand. It was quite anomalous that the driver – with his benign, unremarkable looks – was playing this kind of music. There was something a touch diabolical about it – Urich thought.

Urich was unable to forward-think, to plan in advance. His nerves had scrambled his brains. All he could do was just sit there and let the driver drive. He wondered if he should do something heroic, or if it was expedient to just do nothing.

Before too long, the driver had taken the car into a service station, and parked in the forecourt of a Burger King restaurant. Urich had no idea where they were, and looked out of his window for clues. After clearing his throat, the man got out of the car. "I need to find a loo," he announced, quite matter-of-fact. He appeared to be unbothered at leaving Urich and Cynthia alone in the car.

Urich looked at Cynthia, who had been very quiet for the last hour and she watched his face for a while. She seemed a bit catatonic. Like she had just had a lobotomy. (Though, strangely enough, Urich considered that there was something quite alluring about her in that state.)

Urich and Cynthia watched the man as he became a speck in the distance. A speck with a need to go to the loo.

"What shall we do?" Said Urich.

Cynthia didn't answer; she just clambered into the driving seat, looked underneath the steering wheel and fiddled about for what seemed like about four minutes.

She appeared to know what she was doing, which baffled Urich. What the hell did a woman like Cynthia know about starting up a car?

"Yess!!"

The car was purring again. She had started it up, and was now reversing it at great speed.

"Looks like The Detective is going to have to detect his own car," Cynthia exclaimed.

Urich looked at Cynthia and was stunned by her unexpected sense of calm. He saw her (cool as a cucumber) reverse the car, do a three-point turn and drive the car back onto the motorway.

It was at this point, that Urich did something very odd and very stupid.

Urich was confused clearly, and – also quite apparently – was experiencing an immense feeling of relief. Well, he had just escaped from the clutches of a man who was probably not to be trusted (even though his supposed 'clutch' hadn't been that tight). But while Cynthia tried her hardest to get the both of them the hell away… …..he placed his hand on the front of her cashmere jumper, and Cynthia looked down, slightly surprised. Within a few extra seconds, he had the palm of his hand inside the jumper, and after initially being surprised that she wasn't wearing a bra: was cupping her left breast. He could feel her nipple and had convinced himself that she was enjoying the experience as much as he was.

The car began to swerve and Cynthia, mouthing something unintelligible, seemed momentarily in a state of panic. That was until she elbowed Urich in the side of his head.

"Shit!" said Urich, and it had become clear that Cynthia was not panicking, and was perfectly in control.

Cynthia's face was pale and her eyes, despite Urich's sudden lust, were no longer distracted. They were insane with concentration: absorbed with the substantial task in hand. And Urich now understood this.

"What the hell were you doing!" she said.

Urich did not know what he was doing and could not properly explain his actions. He supposed, in a way, that he was in a dream. It was some kind of sanity-preserving moment; maybe like comfort eating, or being given a nice present when you're feeling down. Something to make things more normal, sort of...

"You really are a STUPID FUCKING CUNT!!"

She kept driving, and Urich detected a faint smile play on her red lips.

"...BUT I swear I will give you what you want just as soon as I know we are safe...OK. Now just sit still! You bloody child!"

Good old Cynthia Price Denning.

She had come full circle and was back to her normal self.

CHAPTER NINETEEN

Once in London: Kings Cross to be exact, Cynthia parked up in a side street, by some rundown hotel, and said she'd be back soon.

Urich wound down the window of the red Nissan and smelled the night air – which was a welcome amalgam of cigarette smoke, weed and chargrilled burgers. There was the comforting sight of pervy tourists, groups of adolescents and dodgy-dealer types. He could hear an argument in the near distance, with expletives and car doors being slammed.

He checked his jacket pockets and pulled his mobile out – and, right at that moment, it started to ring. Urich was unsure if he should answer it. But the phone's din was sending him mad, so he pressed the OK button, anticipating the worst...

"Who is this?"

"It's me. The Detective."

Urich scrunched up his eyes in regret.

"What do you want?" Urich said weakly.

"I told you I want to help you."

"You...."

"Or to be exact, my employer wants me to help you. That is my very specific instruction. And by the way, I have Cynthia...who is safe."

Urich's brain went suitably fuzzy and he didn't know what to say. In films, they would ask to speak to the girl, demanding it…but he wasn't quite sure.

"Put her on!" he said, angrily – secretly wondering if that really was a good thing to do. Urich put his mobile phone flat against his ear and could hear the slightly garbled, electronic tone of Cynthia.

"Jonathan, I think he's speaking the truth. I really do. I think he's on our side!"

Urich needed to ascertain if she was being 'genuine', or if she had been 'persuaded'. But his intense fear made it hard for him to distinguish. In fact, the one thing he could decide on was this: he had to cooperate with this man. It was imperative that he do nothing to endanger Cynthia's life.

(And then he wondered how the hell The Detective could have got into London so quickly. That was quite strange.)

The Detective now informed Urich that it was Carpov who was solely responsible for everything. He said that his employer was onto Carpov and knew how to handle him. The Detective said that it was the publicity of the Zinner acquisition that had brought Carpov to the surface, like "the rain brings spiders into peoples' houses".

OK. Urich thought the last bit to be kind of scary, but felt a certain honesty filter through the electronic airwaves into his ear. His instinct was to trust The Detective, and he made him promise not to harm Cynthia.

"Right, if you're ready to trust me then I can begin to help you," said The Detective.

The Detective's advice was extensive and specific. He would, first of all, need to open the glove compartment and find the spare keys to the Nissan.

Then he told Urich where to cut his hair, purchase the black hair dye and where to shop for clothes. Urich was to undergo a transformation. Soon, he would "become invisible" – whatever that was supposed to mean.

He was to go to a pub called The Devonshire Arms, in Camden – where it was essential that he blend in with other people.

Now, as The Detective explained to a bemused Urich, The Devonshire Arms was a pub specifically for Gothic clientele. If you didn't dress up, you simply were not allowed in.

The Detective explained that at the Devonshire Arms, Urich must hide amongst the regulars. He said it was suitably dark in there. He said it was the kind of place where if you hung out there long enough, normal society would probably forget about you. Forget that you ever existed.

"Are you having a bloody laugh?" exclaimed Urich.

The Detective became quite irate at this; and requested – with a firmness, that Urich found belittling – to never ever question his plans again.

The Detective didn't need to say much else. It was the tone of his voice that let Urich know that he wasn't fooling around. Besides, Urich also had his own reasons for wanting to duck the world's radar.

He approved of the idea, however cranky it seemed. He would become a ghost – metaphorically speaking – and this would be perfect for someone in Jonathan Urich's unique and curious situation.

CHAPTER TWENTY

Urich thought the shaven-headed barman looked pretty *normal* despite a smattering of black eyeliner and a cut-off-sleeves T-shirt. But it wasn't the barman who needed to pass as being authentically alternative. It was Urich.

The cockney barman took one more look at Urich and appeared to be unimpressed. Although Urich had dyed his hair as black as coal, and wore leather trousers – the overall effect of his disguise must have been wrong. Urich supposed this from the over-familiar way the barman was eyeing him – looking for reasons, probably, why Urich should need to be excluded from this place. This safest of places.

But maybe Urich was just over-thinking, being paranoid.

The barman eventually served him and that was that.

He had passed the test.

They had mainly black hair like him – the clientele – which made them look out of sorts; unwell. They seemed generally depressed: both the men and women, despite being in each other's company.

Urich cast a fastidious eye over his attire and was already disappointed: his leather trousers, for starters, were not tight enough;

nor did he have an aura that suggested that he was most definitely on the fringes of society. He appeared too regular, not edgy enough.

He needed to have the merest soupçon of menace about him. So he decided to smile less and, on occasion, snarl very subtly.

He would not, of course, draw too much attention to himself as that might blow his chances of....

His chances of what?

Momentarily confused, he knew that the object of the exercise was to lay low, in order to survive; and with some luck, receive further instructions from The Detective.

In the meantime, he would sit in a dark corner and drink some lager.

As a bed, the red Nissan was wholly uncomfortable. It gave him neck and back-ache which made him despair of the whole operation. Although every time he did query all this: he laughed to himself and thought of worse alternatives.

It was imperative, according to the Detective's previous advice, to stay fully immersed in the role. So he spent the next day walking around Camden – looking in shops and markets, and trying to feel more 'outside of things'. Occasionally, he got the impression that people were laughing at him. And why wouldn't they? His white shirt with frilly sleeves was kitsch; his Kung Fu slippers were a size too small. The new leather trousers, bought to replace the old ones, were so dangerously tight that he could barely walk a few yards without squeaking.

was going to ask Urich to leave, because, most probably, Urich didn't fit in. But something else happened.

He said quite the opposite:

"Ar Proprieta would lav to meet yer."

Urich put down his pint of Pentangle ale and wiped his mouth free of the froth from the pint.

"Your Proprietor?"

"Mista Grimmal."

"Mr Grimmel?"

"Mista Grimmal. He'd leyek to see ya up derr stares," said the barman, sounding less cockney, and more braindamaged.

Urich wondered what this Mr Grimmel wanted with him.

The barman accompanied Urich up the wooden staircase, holding a lit candle.

Urich feared the worst, but went along with the request. He followed the barman into a room on the top landing and felt his head swim a little. He was already nervous.

Urich entered a small dark room with very little furniture. To the right, there was a small bed with crumpled dirty white sheets and a nearby table. On the table, which was white in colour, was a lamp that was turned off.

Further inside the room, in the corner, there was a tall man, standing with his back to them. Urich noticed that he was a thin man with long marmite-coloured hair.

"This is im," said the barman. "The Proprietah!"

Urich watched intently as this tall man turned round – slowly, as if to increase the tension – and faced them both. He was wearing a pair of over-sized dark shades and a tight black vest with the word *Disease* scrawled on it. He walked slowly in tiny steps, as though he had just shat himself.

"You wanted to see me," said Urich, starting to feel a little surreal, and not quite there.

"Yes, so I did," said the Proprietor.

The proprietor then asked to see Urich's mobile phone, which he snatched from Urich and quickly slid into the back pocket of his leather trousers. He sneered at Urich with yellow rotten teeth.

Urich said nothing, as he didn't quite know what to say. He was aware that his mouth had been open for a long time, and his jaw felt quite heavy. The earlier drunken feeling had long since passed.

"I hear you are a man of letters," whispered the Proprietor, sounding more confident of his influence over his guest.

"Letters?"

Urich was transfixed by the way this especially strange man moved, as if every movement was being choreographed by someone else. Someone, perhaps, who was slightly unwell themselves.

"There is something I'd like you to read."

"Er…is there?"

The Proprietor seemed piqued by Urich's reluctance to become involved with his own deeply personal endeavour. Urich could see him clench his fists. Become irked.

Urich began to fidget, tapping the side of his leg. He was clearly uncomfortable in the presence of both the Proprietor and the barman. And attempted to snarl very subtly – except his face felt inept, his mouth inflexible. *It was probably a good thing, him not*

144

being able to achieve 'the snarl', as it might have been viewed as far too
provocative…

"Well, what, er, is it?"

The Proprietor took an eternity to answer Urich's simple
question.

He stepped closer to Urich, and Urich could smell the tang
of the Proprietor's breath. Urich became worried and stumbled
backwards, into the barman, who was still standing there holding a
candle on a small plate.

"Fack!" Said the Barman "Back orf!".

Urich felt intimidated.

"I want you to read my novel. It's called *Stench of Bear*."

Urich almost laughed. But he knew what was happening to
him was no joke.

"Did you say *Stench of Bear*?"

"Yes, I did say *Stench of Bear*," said the Proprietor, gradually,
and with a sinister timbre to his already peculiar voice.

Urich knew of this *Stench of Bear*. It was a fairytale for
children written by someone who was patently disturbed. Urich
remembered that a writer had sent it to him once. It was violent and
disgusting, and involved the antics of a naïve (and mute) bear who
became involved with witchcraft.

Casually and carefully, Mr Grimmel removed his large
sunglasses, revealing marker-pen-thick black eyeliner. He set them
down on the bed and faced Urich. Still watching Urich, he squinted
slightly – a bit like a cat does when it smiles. But without the obvious
charm that a pet might have when doing such a thing.

"It's such a 'grave' situation isn't it, about old Cynthia?" he stated, chuckling to himself. "And to think that a fine bird like her would want to lay an egg like you?"

It was at this point that the tall ghastly man grabbed his own hair and yanked the whole thing onto the floor! He had been wearing a wig (which, incidentally, wasn't so dissimilar to his actual hair – Urich quickly noticed).

Fuck.

It was HIM. It was Carpov, the nub of Urich's nightmare. This was the person who had been harassing him, blackmailing him. Trying to ruin him.

This was the man who had pretended to be Sime Hunst and who had taken money from him (even though technically Carpov did actually invent the concept of The Unread Manuscript ™).

Smiling quite hideously, Carpov pulled out a small kitchen knife from the pocket of his leather trousers, and pointed it in the direction of his guest.

"You're pathetic," said Carpov, sounding slightly East European. He began wildly slashing at the air with the knife, and growling.

Urich looked at the barman and Carpov; and then realised that this was a terrible situation to be in. He wished so desperately not to die, and saw his parents and other aspects of his life flash before his blurring eyes. He even saw his fantasies with Cynthia elapse.

"Don't hurt me," Urich said.

"I won't hurt you you pretty young friend..I will massacre

you, you Shitler!!"

And then Urich, panicking, remembered the advice of Hinds. Hinds had told him that he must say a person's name...but the fuzziness, this mental fog, wouldn't let Urich remember...

"Eugene....no ..Alexander...no....."

Then it came to him: salvation in the form of a memory. Standing proud, he uttered the words, and prayed to himself and to God for results.

"TERENCE RATTIGAN!"

Carpov stopped dead in his tracks and clasped his face, as if something had gotten into his eye socket. He began blinking furiously behind shaking hands.

"Euurrgghhh!!"

Carpov began to stare at his own fist – as if he were willing it to come alive and think for itself, operate outside of his own jurisdiction. He descended to his knees, and, head bowed, spoke in a careful measured voice.

"So you want to play it that way?" Carpov said, smirking at his now raised and tightly-clenched fist. He then stood up and kicked Urich in the face with a black platform boot. With Urich now on his knees, Carpov then grabbed him by the hair – pulling him up onto his feet, in a breathtaking show of strength.

"Please no," complained Urich, but it was too late.

Carpov had pushed his head against a wall, and Urich, punch-drunk, could see stars. Tons of them.

"Take that you evil shitler! You fucking bear pimp!"

Urich knew that he was not yet concussed, but needed to

weather the multiple blows submitted to him by these maniacs. He needed to survive! Perhaps, he hoped, they might tire or get bored... and then they began biting and scratching him.

Carpov, yodelling some kind of bloodcurdling cry, started to rabbit punch Urich on the back of his head. Urich's vision darkened as the wailing, mewing and 'peculiar swearing' became a symphony of hellishness.

Carpov, stopped screaming and began to parade a serrated knife in front of Urich's retreating face. The barman, who was stationary, seemed silently amused at the sight of Carpov taunting his victim.

Urich, who was now lying prostrate on the floor, flinched as Carpov, in some kind of trance, stuck a knife into the floorboards, narrowly missing his arm.

Urich screamed.

"What yer fackin do dat four?" the barman said angrily. Carpov seemed nonplussed, shaken by his own actions.

"He was a good egg was he not...but a little cracked," Carpov said, massaging his own forehead. The barman shrugged his shoulders and appeared to be confused by Carpov.

Something had happened. Had a sense of sanity prevailed?

Things, now, had calmed and the momentum of their violence had slowed to a stop. Andrei Carpov and the (oddly concerned) barman left Urich, doubled up in agony, inside the room. As they left, the door was locked and bolted behind them.

Urich could still hear both men bickering outside, discussing Carpov's behaviour. He was worried and paced the room, moaning loudly like a child.

All he could think of was escaping. He looked around the windowless room and saw nothing of interest to him. The walls were white and Urich remembered how white walls, alone, could drive someone insane.

CHAPTER TWENTY-ONE

It had been about two days, or at least Urich thought. The room was cold and lonely, and – despite not having a window – he could hear Camden outside; which made him feel less estranged. If he listened hard he could hear cars and buses and people talking; sometimes laughing.

He had begun talking to himself occasionally. Or, sometimes, he had sung a little – in an effort to keep his spirits up and try to remain sensible. How long was he to be incarcerated here? He wondered if singing was a preventative measure, or an actual symptom of madness.

He wondered if he would die here.

The incessantly white room was beginning to get to him, and his intense boredom had made him more than aware of the visual irony of being dressed all in black inside a totally white room.

He banged on the door, and shouted with all the voice he had left inside him.

"LET ME OUT OF HERE YOU PSYCHO!" WHY DO THIS TO ME!"

And then something strange happened. Urich had awoken from a brief sleep, and saw a manuscript on the floor, similar to the one he had found in Hunst's flat. It appeared to be the exact same thing – apart from two differences.

The first difference was that the title (*"The Confessions"*) had been scribbled out in pencil. Above the crossed-out title was a new moniker: *"A Nasty Line In Work: The Diary of Liz Weston. (Third Draft)"*.

The second difference was that the blue-bound manuscript had been punched with a rather large hole on the left margin, middle section. Through this hole was a piece of greyish string that lead out from under the locked door.

Urich, cautiously, dropped to his hands and knees and inspected the new manuscript and reached out a hand to touch it. Before he could touch the thing, someone from outside the door had tugged the string so hard that it flew into the base of the door.

Urich heard a growl and someone – unknown to Urich – had asked that Urich stand in the corner of the room and shut his eyes. The voice – a low, assertive gasp of a voice – asked him to obey the instructions. It sounded like Carpov, but it just might have been someone else.

Urich did exactly this, and heard the door being unlocked with a loud click and impressive clunk. He heard footsteps and, quicker than expected, heard the door close again and the sound of a key fumble about in the lock. The manuscript was gone.

This never happened again.

After perhaps the third day, he woke up and wondered if he had been drugged. He felt that his thoughts seemed housed in the wrong head: illogical, unfamiliar. He felt faint, detached from his surroundings.

Then footsteps outside the door again; the door was being unlocked with the same thunderous and jolting noise.

Urich rose from his sitting position on the (white) floor – his eyes busy, his senses hectic. This time, though, there was no one behind the door. So, with haste, he pulled open the door, ran out and flew down the wooden staircase.

There were quite a few people in the downstairs pub – Goths, obviously. And no one seemed to notice him as he shook his head from side to side, wildly checking to see if he was being pursued.....until he tripped over someone's long, pointy boot near the bar. A few heads turned, but most continued to listen to the song that was playing on the jukebox, and drink beer.

Finally, he ran into the night air and clenched his fists in celebration.

He was free. He was not going to die unloved, or be tortured. His life was his, to live freely.

He went to the side road, across the road, where he had parked the red Nissan and saw that it was still there. He unlocked the car door, with the spare key, and sat in the driver's seat.

His mobile phone was sitting there on the dashboard.

With trepidation, he picked the phone up and scrolled down his contact list. He needed desperately to try and call Cynthia. But something was wrong.

All numbers in his address book had been erased. Except for one, and that was Zinner's. It was his personal number, his mobile number.

Why Zinner's number…or had Carpov left that number purely by mistake? Although Urich knew that it would be prudent not to ring the number, he did exactly that. He rang it, knowing that he couldn't call the police.

With unease, he dialled the number and a voice answered.

"Jonathan, I've been meaning to speak with you."

"Zinner," Urich said breathlessly. "I need to know is Cynthia OK? Has anything happened to her?"

"Jonathan, as far as I know Cynthia is alright."

"I need you to hide me," said Urich. "I'm experiencing a few problems…."

Zinner was warm and understanding, and asked Urich to drop by the gallery as soon as possible.

When Zinner saw the frenzied agent – complete with feminine make-up and raven-black hair…...he tried to remain straight-faced. Whilst trying not to laugh, Zinner's eyes became a little too focused and intense, which was off-putting to Urich.

"Hinds has explained your incredible situation," said Zinner.

Urich was curious and suspicious, and would play his cards close to his chest. He would not mention anything about Monty Carn. He just wanted safety first and foremost. In fact, he really wanted food. He was starving and was on the verge of fainting, or hallucinating.

"I do want to help you," added Zinner.

"I don't want the police involved. I can't explain, but I just don't," Urich blurted out, over-breathing. He was giddy, again, because of his hunger; and he regretted his outspokenness.

Zinner escorted him into the main hall of his gallery, and Urich almost keeled over. Centrally positioned was a steel cage with bars. Inside the cage, which measured about 10 by 7 feet, was a toilet, a small bed, a Baby Belling cooking facility and some spare sheets and bedding material. It was like a bed-sit.

"What the fuck is that? I don't understand," said Urich.

"This is somewhere where you will be safe from Carp. Somewhere that will be expertly guarded...there are cameras, witnesses, people."

"But for how long?"

"Just a few days or a week. Think about it? After the robbery of the 'The Unread Manuscript ™', this will be the safest, most expertly guarded place on the planet. What are the chances of Carp ever getting to you? And if he does turn up, then we can pounce on him, right?"

Zinner asked him to think about the offer of 'security', and told him about the gastronomic delights on offer. Food cooked by celebrity chefs, Burger King, whatever he wanted. Every single day. When he wanted it.

Zinner didn't stop at pleasures of the culinary kind.

"I will give you as much cocaine as your nose can handle... to make your stay a bit more bearable. Art simply doesn't have to adhere to the same laws as everyone else. Art is a superior host and a most flexible employer."

And Urich could not think of anything else but the severed head in the boot of his car and Carpov trying to stab him. But then, flashing on and off inside his head: that footage of the girl dead, with URICH holding a knife to her throat...

"I'll do it," said Urich.

Zinner pulled out a scrunched-up piece of paper from his back pocket. He straightened it out upon a raised knee – whilst standing on one foot.

"Sign this then. It's just a standard form."

Urich glanced at it and walked away from Zinner.

"What's the deal? he asked coolly. "Obviously, I know you are going to make me some kind of live exhibit. I'm not that stupid."

"And what would be so bad about that," said Zinner quietly. "Maybe you could become the kind of commodity you are more used to selling. You, Mr Urich, could become art."

Urich thought quickly and knew that Zinner was playing him for a fool. He had read Burgundy Conew's (rather excellent) *ARTexplained* and knew about codes and metaphors and flip social comments.

Zinner – Urich suggested to himself – was trying to make a statement about offensive machinations and sterile bureaucratic worlds that people like Urich inhabited – as opposed to the self-imposed prisons that artists (those martyrs!) lived in, or something.

(Somehow being hungry and barely conscious had sharpened up his thinking skills, considerably.)

But Zinner interrupted Urich's new and impressive thinking.

"I have a rather good idea too. When Cynthia is delivered

back to us. You and her will stay together in a gesture of harmony...
in this cage. It will be a brilliant, upbeat conclusion to recent events."

Urich, in a split-second, had realised what Zinner
had wanted him and Cynthia to be doing. He foresaw himself
gloriously (yet romantically) making love to Cynthia, in front of an
entranced audience.

Clever bastard – Urich suddenly realised.

Of course, Zinner was making a flip visual statement about
the agent *fucking* the 'artist'. But Urich had never fucked or screwed
anyone for money. He had treated writers decently.

Then Urich got to thinking. Really thinking – candidly.

He imagined the rapture, the almighty release that being
with Cynthia would bring to him. He thought, again, of crowds
cheering him on – roaring with art patriotism, chanting his name.
Urich! Urich! Urich!

He thought of the drabness of the literary scene: the middle-
aged, wrinkled, like-my-parentness of it all. The flatulent egos and
paucity of good fun and drugs.

Then he thought of ART.

Then he, again, returned to: Cynthia's face – ecstatic,
blissful, flushed with the divinity of just having had sex with
someone like the newly artistic Jonathan Urich. Then he remembered the all too real threat of the psychopath Andrei Carpov. (And
visualised Hinds and Cynthia at his funeral, slow-clapping the casket
as they carried his dead body out....)

Then he foresaw safety in numbers. He dreamed of big
crowds and nestling his clean-shaven face into Cynthia's modest but

safe bosom. He would be protected from harm in Zinner's small circus. It was safety incarnate, this: Zinner's option.

The cage seemed like a very good idea.

An only idea.

He grabbed the form from out of Zinner's hand, and demanded that he be given a pen.

CHAPTER TWENTY-TWO

Tonight the world could view Ernest Zinner's latest acquisition in the Zinner Arcade, Kensington. It was a palatial space with everything from empty boxes to wall-high Rothko's. There were miniature water-fountains with pink water spurting forth, and ironic paintings of Princess Diana.

The rock music (Primal Scream, Elton John, some Texas) formed a sonic wind and blew gently over the muzak of a thousand similar conversations. Waitresses danced around with plates of canapés in their small hands; and the champagne flowed. Everyone from the gallery smiled; many of the guests didn't – as smiling, of course, made people look naïve. Then, too quickly, the music stopped and an audible drone began: as if a swarm of bees had descended on the evening.

A group of five male assistants, in lab coats, wheeled in a super-large construction that had a series of grey flannel sheets preventing anyone from seeing what was inside.

A lurid blast of twisted, almost-psychedelic death metal came from out of unseen speakers; and then the grey flannel sheets were swiftly removed.

There was Urich.

Inside a twenty-foot high, aluminium cage – but surrounded

by a layer of perspex glass inside the steel bars. And a crowd was gathering around him as the effects of a sleeping tablet were wearing off.

Urich gathered his thoughts and fought to be clearheaded. It was cramped, and stuffy where he was, and he didn't like everyone looking at him.

He had heard what had been said. He was especially confused why they were calling the exhibit, this piece of modern art: 'Therapist' (as a placard across the room was advertising it). He just didn't get it. Why was the exhibit called 'Therapist'? Were they implying that he was not in his right mind? Was this about trying to help him?

And then he saw them:

Cynthia, Mr Hinds and….. '*Oh Jesus Christ!?*'; his eyes must have been playing tricks on him...a hallucination?

(*Or was he in hell?*)

It was Monty Carn. *(The full Monty – complete with head!!*)

He was alive, well and greeting a clearly emotional Ernest Zinner. They were shaking hands and embracing with slaps upon backs, and callous laughter that was muted because of the glass wallpaper of Urich's cage.

Although pissed, Carn was carrying himself with more poise than he had ever done previously. It seemed that he'd lost weight and, somehow, had acquired a suit that actually fitted.

Carn approached the new exhibit and stared in amazement. He stepped forward, edging past a group of astounded Swedish onlookers.

"Oh, this is good!" Carn muttered to himself. Despite his jollity, he was still unable to make eye contact with Urich, even as he chucked some peanuts at the glass, from a source in his blazer pocket.

"Oh, the monkey has been climbing again and has taken a nasty fall!" Carn's strident voice was deafening; like kryptonite to Urich's weakened state.

Monty Carn continued: "And it looks like, once again, Peter Pan has got 'played' by a woman!"

Cynthia, who was listening, smiled at this; and appeared to be embarrassed.

Monty Carn guffawed and chortled, excessively; and made light of Urich's unconcealed pain. For the first time in his life, Urich had felt a tremendous sensitivity towards...well, towards himself.

Why, though, could no one see his anguish?

Urich lifted his head and could see that Carn and Cynthia were now holding hands, and appeared to be uninterested in him. He shook his head and stared at the floor. He had been in the cage for three days and had not been given one single idea of when he would be allowed to leave. Neither had they given him all the things they said they were going to give him.

"Let me out?" he asked, weakly, of no one in particular. He could only manage a whisper. "Now, seriously, please, let me out..."

His voice was thin, barely a rasp.

It was imperative that he make eye-contact with Cynthia, but she was too far away.

Against his will, he started to weep; at first, without

producing tears: a kind of dry-retch of emotion. And before too long, he cried uncontrollably: a surge of saltwater tears, and a great yawning sorrow, the like of which he had never experienced before. He didn't care who saw him. But at the back of his mind, he wondered if Cynthia would notice and feel concern.

If she had been looking: she would have seen the misery piss out constantly from his eyes, making a small lake on the metal floor of his cage. If he had been able to look back at her, he would have noticed her eyes: distinctly dry.

Then another guest arrived.

Urich's arched, aching back straightened in disgust at the sight of Andrei Carpov, who had just come into view...

Carpov was wearing aviator sunglasses and had his dirty grey hair slicked right back. He wore a white string vest, and draped upon his awful frame was a long brown leather coat that brushed the floor as he walked. His fingers were painted with black nail varnish; and red lipstick was pasted thickly upon his wrinkled arsehole of a mouth.

Carpov was uncomfortable and fidgety. He stared at Urich in the cage and growled quietly to himself.

Zinner – wearing sandals, red slacks and a black waistcoat – greeted Carpov with zest, and whispered something in his ear. Scanning the room, he waited for his moment, and dropped something into the side-pocket of Carpov's leather coat.

Carpov smiled knowingly to himself. It was time for the great actor to become even more fully immersed in his role.

Sensing that a nearby waitress was looking at him, and detecting her discomfort – he walked over to her. He craned his head down and spoke softly into her ear.

"Do you know that I am to take the stage soon, my sweet bear...and I am to enter that cage and what I have been paid to do to Mr Urich will make him surely pass out..."

He showed her a small silver key that was to give him access to the cage. The fair-haired waitress said nothing, and made small steps backward – smiling apologetically.

Zinner came out of the rotunda and stepped onto the balcony – and looking down on his audience, he grabbed the microphone to make an announcement. His amplified voice was great and powerful, and instead of his usually dour face...there was a new emotion present: resentment, passion perhaps.

Everyone: artists, critics, models, accountants, students – looked up and anticipated something exciting.

"In the event of last month's robbery, I thought it would only be right to give you something a little bit shocking. Some might say that this is both edgy and sexually neurotic. THIS is the story of a man....with ideas above his station...who escaped the safe solitary world of books to enjoy the unbridled, universal, all encompassing orgy that is Art and what art stands for. He did nothing wrong. And he probably blames himself...but IT IS NOT REALLY ABOUT HIM! Without understanding, he dared to fuck with art...but Art, who didn't like that, decided to fuck well and truly with him!!

"Ladies and Gentleman and art lovers alike I give you a conceptual exhibit...and some of the more sensitive of you might

162

want to look away, or retire to the next room..

"..THE RAPIST!"

And many stood there – unsure if the exhibit would be as disgusting and scandalous as the rumour mill had suggested. Would the conceptual art piece 'The Rapist (or What Doesn't Kill You... Might, In Fact, Rape You Instead)', to quote its full title, really deliver the goods?

Many were perplexed by the art piece that hadn't quite happened. Others were prematurely outraged. Andrei James Carpov – who found it all a bit philosophically weak – was unimpressed with all this prattle; and fiddled, purposefully, with the large cage key inside his coat pocket; and imagined his part in the exhibit, and how to push boundaries. What he needed to do was simple: sicken his audience.

That was the brief. His artistic licence.

"So come on down, Mr Carpov!" announced Zinner, and that was Carpov's cue.

And – although Carpov considered himself to be different from the others, he was also on the payroll, just like the others. And needed to impress.

But he wondered though: was this just a stepping stone to something else, or was it 'this' that he was passionate about?

The crowd, just as Carpov had hoped, gave a big cheer just as he turned the key in the lock...

Downstairs, in Zinner's private office, the chief players in the 'strategy' congratulated each other. It had seemed an impossible feat to pull off – but also quite easy. No one, in their wildest dreams, had thought that Urich would actually agree to go in the cage – especially of his own accord. (As a result of this, they had even abandoned a phase of the operation.)

They talked about method acting, Lee Strasberg and psychology. And deconstructed Urich being in the cage, and saw how – as a unit – they had all created art that was stimulating, and commercial.

Urich, you see, was art. BUT where was the artist? They had bypassed the artist, of course. So this meant they had to pay one less person.

But that was the way things were probably going – cutting out middlemen. Artists were difficult and impulsive prima donnas, who asked too high a price.

Without fail.

Hinds, drinking champagne from a thin glass, had later explained, that "both the devil and God are in the detail, and the small print is for angels as well as knaves."

Everybody had agreed with him.

Both The Thief and The Girl had been absent from this particular evening.

The Thief had not been invited on account of his Employer's latest request.

(*And how these requests had increased in frequency.*)

The Thief, at the last minute, had been required to bury

"some bad news" in the New Forest. It was another obscure and sickening task that was better left undescribed.

The Thief – a mild-mannered man, who questioned little – was annoyed initially; but accepted that, at least, he was earning money. Good money.

And a job, whatever it consisted of, was still a job.

Whereas The Girl: she was sadly absent for the very significant reason that she had been dead a long time: ever since that first night, to be exact.

Prostitution had been her particular profession. (But, in secret: she had been writing, in a diary, the honest and heartrending story of her own life, which no one would ever read.)

EPILOGUE

Zinner, in a rare act of kindness, had given him a laptop computer and it was everything to him now. But would people would want to read about Urich and his recent tribulations?

At least, for his sanity's sake, he hoped they would.

This writing project was his salvation now:

an antidote to a rather horrible future.

It had been a month.

Urich was still in the cage; and had awoken from a dream where he was starving and had eaten a dismembered ear that someone had thrown to him. In the ghastly dream, he found the small meal nourishing.

It had been a month, in the cage.

People found this bearded dishevelled man disturbing and, in return, he found their interest heartbreaking. Soul-destroying. He had become famous – everything that he had dreamed of...and all he wanted, now: was anonymity, privacy.

He just wanted to take a shit without people staring at him.

On the positive side, though, he had been given the formal news that a buyer was interested in him, and wondered if he would be set free.

HE WONDERED:

Would the new buyer be compassionate, human even?

Or would he just be a cunt, interested in nothing but his investment?

....

On the phone to Zinner was The Thief's Employer.

An end was in sight.

A deal was about to be struck.

The Employer was tickled by Zinner's acquisition, and now wanted it for himself. It was due to him, of course. It always had been.

He hadn't thought much about which house it should be placed in: Cannes, Primrose Hill, Santa Monica. (Though he'd worry about Feng Shui, and consequences, at a later date.)

"So Sime, it is all yours now," said Zinner. "As agreed, you will pay me my fee."

The artist Sime Hunst (the original one, and not the forgery) said nothing, and was already bored.

Another acquisition would not slake the visionary's thirst for the mind-blowing and the life-changing effect that art could really have on a person's soul.

Another acquisition could never fully replace that need to shake the world up. That need to turn things upside down...

THIS was not enough.

You see, cruelty and lesson-teaching were in vogue these days. And would be for the foreseeable future.

(In a cerebal montage, his mind conjured images of multiple murders and death on a grand scale, terrorism and horrors too impossible to navigate through.)

After he'd put down the receiver, Hunst poured himself a mineral water and, questioning the point of life briefly, paused.

Then became lifeless,

still-life,

a statue.

THE

END....